MASK BY MASK

Tyler Kyle

BALBOA. PRESS

A DIVISION OF HAY HOUSE

Balboa Press books may be ordered through booksellers or by contacting:

Balboa Press
A Division of Hay House
1663 Liberty Drive
Bloomington, IN 47403
www.balboapress.com
1 (877) 407-4847

Because of the dynamic nature of the Internet, any web addresses or links contained in this book may have changed since publication and may no longer be valid. The views expressed in this work are solely those of the author and do not necessarily reflect the views of the publisher, and the publisher hereby disclaims any responsibility for them.

The author of this book does not dispense medical advice or prescribe the use of any technique as a form of treatment for physical, emotional, or medical problems without the advice of a physician, either directly or indirectly. The intent of the author is only to offer information of a general nature to help you in your quest for emotional and spiritual well-being. In the event you use any of the information in this book for yourself, which is your constitutional right, the author and the publisher assume no responsibility for your actions.

Any people depicted in stock imagery provided by Thinkstock are models, and such images are being used for illustrative purposes only.
Certain stock imagery © Thinkstock.

Print information available on the last page.

ISBN: 978-1-5043-7132-2 (sc)
ISBN: 978-1-5043-7131-5 (hc)
ISBN: 978-1-5043-7133-9 (e)

Library of Congress Control Number: 2016920236

Balboa Press rev. date: 02/07/2017

Sometimes you just need to eat spaghetti and fuck.

Everything will be okay.

The mirror reflected books alone. Books of every size and color filled the ceiling-height bookcase, which ran the length of the stone wall. More books spilled out from underneath the bed. She counted the reflection of the bookshelves over and over, stopping when she reached seven only to begin again, the countless, nameless pages a mystery. All the books had been placed backward on the shelves, their titles hidden from view. The white, cream, yellow, and brown pages spoke nothing to the counting young woman, whose long blonde hair was streaked with dried blood.

She held her throbbing head, sat up in the bed to lean back against the warm leather headboard, and counted the shelves once more. Haunting chords of a guitar penetrated the bedroom through the closed door. One, two, three, four—a small bouquet of orange roses in a squatty earthen vase. Five, six, seven—the deep brown monogram on the crisp white sheets. The music of the guitar stopped suddenly, and she realized she had no idea what the letters on the pillowcase stood for.

Ada washed her face with cold water before looking up into the mirror. She coerced a loose curl over the faint, jagged scar that ran the length of her temple at her hairline. She forced her practiced smile as she stared into her blue eyes. It was nothing she could not handle now, only a dream—a dream she had not dreamed for several years, yet a dream no less. Ada was still right to have come. She settled back into the oversize bed and pulled the orange satin quilt up over her chest before clicking off the glass lamp. One, two, three—an orange petal—four, five, six, seven. Ada sat up again to turn the lamp back on. The large diamond on her finger snagged the sheets as she leaned against the cold, dark wood of the headboard. She ran her finger down the orange satin stripe of the pillowcase to finally trace her own initials onto the crisp white sheets. It was only the jet lag. She was right to have come.

The apartment was luxurious, calculated in its location and excessive dimensions to remind Ada of all that she had become in the last ten years. Having passed the sleepless night staring down at Las Ramblas from her top-story window, Ada now unpacked her large Louis Vuitton suitcases, sipping a *café con leche* between hanging up dresses. She organized her rows of sandals and stilettos by color in the large, cedar-paneled closet before finally falling back on the stark white coverlet of the king-size bed. Ada lit a cigarette and sighed. She had changed rooms after the dream the night before. This grand bedroom, with its dark, exposed wooden beams overhead and lonely orange leather chair, was not quite as pretty as her first choice but provided large windows that overlooked the street below nonetheless. Ada knew she would switch back in a night or so anyway, the two bedrooms in reality unnecessary since she was traveling alone. Though that was precisely the point. All the beds in the apartment were hers. She had paid for them herself.

Ada stood and walked over to the window. She pushed a curl out of her face and then untied her thin robe. She stared down at the serpentine green of trees along the street below. Barcelona. It had been ten years. She never imagined she would dare to come back, and yet she felt somehow she owed it to herself. This was the only way to convince herself of who she was—that it was not just an illusion. For now the paper-wrapped journal remained hidden safely inside the drawer of the nightstand in the other bedroom. Ada would never really open it, of course, and she now had the stark white bedroom to sleep in when she wanted to be free of all traces of the journal's contents.

"I'm here to do whatever I please," Ada told herself aloud with a huge smile. Her self-assured laugh serenaded the room. She finished her cigarette in silence.

Ada showered in the orange-tiled bathroom. Hot water flowed over her lean, curvy, fatigued body like a waterfall from the ceiling, all orange safely hidden from view as she squeezed her eyes closed. Ada felt strong, powerful, and alive, aside from the vexing orange. She distracted herself with thoughts of citrus groves and Mediterranean sunshine as she slipped on her short skirt. She sought to forget the color orange outside of these contexts. She adjusted her black tank and put on a large, oval onyx ring before deciding to ready herself in the brown-tiled bathroom instead. She had already thrown away the bouquet of orange roses she had found on the sink basin the night before. Of all the apartments to rent in Barcelona, how could she have known that hers would be freshly remodeled in orange? She did her makeup simply—long, dark lashes, a touch of bronzer, and a hint of color on her lips.

After finally tying up her black wedge espadrilles in the living room, Ada grabbed her woven satchel and locked up the apartment. She walked down the five flights of stairs. She had no plans, no commitments for four weeks. Still, there were places she would not dare to go. She willed that her wandering feet be bound by restraint. Deadened memories existed that she would not risk awakening, no matter how confident she had become. She was in Barcelona to prove her strength, not kill herself.

"You would like some company today, miss?" A man on a bicycle rode up alongside her on the sidewalk. He was young, tan, his easy curls blowing as he pedaled to match Ada's long stride.

"No," Ada said. She kept walking. He continued to ride alongside her. She glanced sideways to see her candor had drained the energy of his large grin into slouched shoulders. She sighed impatiently and added, "But thank you."

"Why you are alone?" He spoke in French. He looked her straight in the eyes.

"Because I want to be," Ada answered, annoyed not with the question but with herself for answering it. "I am here to fulfill my grandmother's death wish. I need to focus, please."

"I am very sorry, mademoiselle," he said, "but you are very beautiful. I will help you. I can."

"Good-bye," Ada said as she turned sharply to her right and took an outdoor seat in a café without hesitation. She winked at the waiter who was about to seat the table with an American couple and then promptly ordered an espresso. No one asked her not to smoke. She inhaled as she stared, not seeing the passing tourists. Why the fuck was she explaining herself to anyone? She was here for herself. Period. Not even Paulo had her address. And why the fuck had she said that about her grandmother? Could that be true? After half an hour, Ada got up to stroll down Las Ramblas toward the Mediterranean. She diverted herself with the colorful flower stalls and the warmth of sunshine on her skin until she came to the towering monument to Christopher Columbus at the end. She had intentionally left her camera in the apartment, not admitting to herself that she knew exactly where she was going on her first day back. She turned left to follow Paseo Colon toward Port Vell. Ada stared out across the sea at the collection of boats, following the sidewalk with her shoulders pushed back and her head held high. She refused to look ahead. White boats gleamed in the sunlight, and Ada's eyes smiled behind her large, dark sunglasses. She lost herself for one moment in the impression she'd had the first time she stared out over the port. One, two, three—stumbling on the sidewalk, Ada then had the opportunity to genuinely profess shock. She recovered to find herself staring up across the street at a seven-story apartment building. She gasped, looking every which way about her before laughing. She struggled to see if she could make anything out inside the windows of the upper stories.

"What are you doing here, Ada?" she whispered. Suddenly she had lost her nerve. A man in a suit passed by and stared. "I have every right to be here. It's just for fun. Come on, Ada. Remember who you are."

She turned and thought a moment. She picked up her pace and spent the rest of the afternoon pretending to explore the Gothic Quarter as a tourist, as if she did not know every passageway by heart. She wandered slowly through the streets, running her fingers along the cool stone walls, wishing she had not left her camera behind. Over the last ten years, Ada's camera had become an extension of herself— her eyes by the manner in which she saw life, and her mind by the way she recorded her perspectives. Ada owed her success to her ability to translate motionless images into breathless meaning—life encapsulated in a single frame. As the most sought-after wedding photographer in Northern California, Ada had planned this vacation over a year in advance, nearly ten years to the day of her last visit to Barcelona. That Ada made such a good living from photographing weddings for magazines and for couples across the globe was a great joke among her friends. Ada's left hand was conspicuously bare now as she walked along the half-shaded, half-sunny Calle del Obispo Irurita. She had made herself happy off of other people's love. After a wedding or shoot, she would take a wine or cooking class, meet someone for the weekend, and content herself that love was for other people.

Late in the afternoon, Ada came upon the Cathedral of Saint Eulalia. Its imposing, gothic façade towered against the blue-tinged sky. She searched her satchel in vain for her camera once again. The cathedral was immense, impenetrable, unmoving, as though the soiled gray stone of the apparent fortress ran as deep as the earth's core. Grandma. Ada knew her clothes would not allow her to enter, so she stopped halfway up the stone steps to stare upward again. The intricate spires pierced the sky above, and she felt the heaviness of the solemn base. Her eyes danced as she studied the façade more carefully, saints and symbols, Grandma's lullabies sounding through the crowds on the wind. Without her camera, Ada was losing her accomplished control.

She turned suddenly and stepped on someone's foot. An elderly woman shouted at her in Catalan. Ada rushed down the steps.

"To the office, Ada," Mrs. Dwight said. Her thin lips were taut, her brow deeply wrinkled, yet her hand somehow white and smooth as she handed a pink slip to Ada.

"But," Ada began to plead. She stopped herself. Ada stood up straighter and fell silent to watch Mrs. Dwight take the thick pink pad from her pocket. She wrote the words "disrespectful and argumentative" along the dark, straight line.

"Now you can explain your attitude to Mr. Butler, as well."

Ada walked down the brick walkway, her head held high as she passed the window of her sixth-grade English classroom. She knew she was being watched and started to dance. Her classmates laughed and cheered. Ada bent over and slapped her ass. Mr. Miller came to the window too, but Ada knew he would not do anything. He just watched.

Ada opened the glass door to the office at the front of the tree-lined school. The secretary did not greet her. She never did. She merely held out her hand for the pink slips. Ada sat down on the hard wooden bench and watched the second hand go round and round above on the noisy old clock.

"Come in, Ada," Mr. Butler said. He stared down at her.

Ada stood up and smoothed her plaid skirt out as she walked past him. He closed the heavy oak door behind her. She did not sit in either of the tufted leather chairs in front of his desk. She knew the drill by now.

"Another dress code violation, Ada?" Mr. Butler asked, taking out his ruler from the top drawer of his desk. "Do you have no respect for chapel day?"

"I'm tall, Mr. Butler," Ada said. She stared up into his bearded face. "And why would God create legs if he's so ashamed of them?"

"Insolent girl." Mr. Butler's eyes lit up as he ran his finger along the side of the ruler. "Kneel down."

Ada decided to get it over quickly this time. She wanted to be back in class to meet the new students from Australia. She knelt down, her knees tender on the hard wood planks beneath her. She stared at a spider spinning a web in the corner behind the desk. Why didn't Mr. Butler clean his office? He stood directly in front of her, close enough for her to smell his breath as he bent over. He slid the ruler down her thigh until it touched the floor. He pressed it against her skin and then put his finger on the hem of her skirt. He left it there as Ada waited.

"Ada, do you feel my finger?" Mr. Butler asked. "Your skirt is clearly too short."

Several hours later, after having shopped the Plaza Catalunya, Ada smiled as she set her new black python clutch on the white coverlet of the bed and lit a cigarette. The silence was at first peaceful, then haunting. Ada searched for the phone she had hidden away in the closet and then walked into the living room to lean against the window frame. Her eye followed the winding river of green leaves as the phone rang on the other end.

"Hello."

Ada squeezed her eyes closed and hesitated. She walked over to fall back into a dark, curved chaise lounge before smashing her cigarette into the clear glass ashtray. She cleared her throat. "Hi, it's me."

"I know it's you, and to what do I owe this great, unexpected pleasure?"

"What's that supposed to mean?" Ada asked. She blew the curls out of her eyes before leaning back and staring up at the crystal chandelier.

"You weren't going to call, remember?"

"Well, I just thought you might like to know I got here safely." Ada ran her finger down the chrome leg of the chair.

"I'm glad you're safe, Ada. I only wish you had called last night. I was hoping you would."

"I'm a big girl, Paulo. Worrying is useless."

The prolonged silence was followed by a muffled sigh. "So, how's the apartment?"

"Gorgeous. Huge."

"Well, if it gets too big, I can get out of here. You'd like the family apartment in Madrid."

"I'll be home in a month. I don't know if I'll call again though. I just need a little time alone to think. You know, we're always so busy. Being here makes me realize I haven't stopped to think much in the past ten years."

"Well, I'll miss you, Ada, but as long as you're still wearing your ring, I can wait."

Ada stared at the glass oval coffee table. The five-karat diamond ring glimmered in the light that flooded the room through the large, ceiling-height windows. She breathed deeply as she sat up on the edge of the chair to examine the huge, multifaceted stone.

"Ada? Ada? Ada, you are wearing your ring, aren't you?"

"What kind of a question is that?" Ada laughed. She struggled to slip on the ring as she stood up and walked back over to the windows. "Of course I'm wearing my ring, Paulo. It's amazing, and everyone I know is jealous. What woman wouldn't love having this diamond on her finger? Listen, I need to go get some dinner now. I haven't had much to eat all day."

"It was good hearing your voice, Ada. I love you. Take care of yourself."

"I'll be home soon. Kisses."

Ada turned off her phone. She would not lose her nerve. She locked the phone away in one of her suitcases in the closet and then ventured back out into the hallway to stand in front of the closed door. Ada leaned her head forward onto the dark wood and slipped the diamond off her finger. She opened the door and walked over to sit down on the orange silk coverlet of the unmade bed. She slid open the top drawer of the nightstand and saw the brown paper before looking away. She dropped the ring on top of her journal and hid it away in the darkness.

3

That night Ada could not fall asleep. She tried to read a book, then a magazine. She did a headstand and went through a series of yoga poses. She opened all the windows and then a bottle of Priorat *tinto*. After that, she smoked several cigarettes. Nothing helped. She knew if she were to go down the hall and lie down naked on the sheets of either bed that sleep would not come. She did not even want to be in the same room as the journal. And fuck thinking about Nathan. No, the bed would only cause her to remember more. Ada lay down on the chaise longue and poured another glass of wine. She wished she were back home in her own bedroom. If she were, she would open the shades, burn *papier d'Arménie* and look out to the bridge. It helped her sleep. It made her feel safe.

Granted, the Golden Gate Bridge was an unmistakable symbol. It was like the Eiffel Tower or the Great Wall of China for people. It was internationally recognizable, a supermagnet. Famous, yes, but it was never a cliché. It could not be. It was too stunning, too much a vision of possibility, too frightening. It was the gate to San Francisco and Ada's gate to a new life of her choosing, unexpected as that might have been at the time. And she did well there. She buried every pang, every encounter that reminded her that she did not really belong. It was the weather, deliberately chosen, because in truth, it did not suit her. That was the precisely the point. It gnawed away at her soul bit by bit, hauntingly beautiful, cold, and rigid. Her clothing became stark, modern, simple, and overwhelmingly black. This was not so much a reflection of the city's style as her own sense of self in the north. There was no doubt that she was extremely well turned out, from her flawless skin to her enviable physique to her understated designer labels. She was in complete control, and that was exactly what she wanted. No vacillating, no bumps—just the foggy, dreary weather to keep herself firmly planted in her own willpower.

Barcelona changed things, including memories. From the moment she stepped off the plane, it had opened her back up to warmth.

10

Warmth scared her. So did memories. Warmth was an open invitation for her free spirit to flourish. But she did not want to lose control. She would not falter. She could make it through Barcelona and fly back to California having conquered that wild stallion. She could be elegant, thoroughbred, cool. She would be brave, ruthless—let the memories come, defeat them, and go home and marry Paulo. Then she would live very well, and the past would remain in the past.

Yet the change seemed to have happened suddenly and immediately. Even on the first day, Ada left her hair to the sun and wind. Next she would be curling her hair in ringlets or wearing it wavy. She would vacillate between the classic starlet and hedonistic bohemian that she was in the heat. But the image of the Golden Gate in her mind's eye steadied her. In San Francisco, she wore her hair straight and shiny, perfectly blonde, perfectly put together. Black and neutrals were her staples, literally. They held her together. Her colorful sundresses were stored with her luggage for island holidays. If she kept to her apartment over the weekend, she wore designer jeans, a white tank top, and a warm cashmere wrap to keep the cold out. Yes. She worked, she bought, she celebrated, but all was contained. The fog, the bridge, the cold.

Even if it were a cliché, Ada did not mind it in this instance. Flooded by tourists day in and day out, the Golden Gate Bridge had become the personal symbol of Ada's recent years. It was the bridge that solidified her choice of apartment. The view from her bedroom window was a form of self-medication. As she stared out late at night she reminded herself of why she had come to live there and recited the now familiar list of reasons why it was best for her. In the rare instance when she was completely honest, the bridge was too perfect a choice. It was by far sexy enough to be the facade for the barricade that it was. Bridges were links, and this was her very thin, calculated, showpiece link to a life that she preferred an ocean to divide. The plan was a good one. She never had to see herself as a runaway—just a woman who had evolved into controlled power over her life. It was a good one, after all.

Beauty, sex, suicide, life, and death. The bridge was all to Ada. Unlikely savior. Kate was the only one who knew anything about her, and not even she knew very much.

"No, I've never fucked anyone for money. I used to wish that I could, but I just can't."

Kate was Ada's first and best friend in San Francisco. They were snowed in for the weekend. Lake Tahoe. Kate's boyfriend's cabin. He was on a guy's trip down the coast. Ada and Kate had come to the cabin to ski that weekend. Instead they passed the time practicing yoga, getting high, reading erotic poetry in the hot tub, and making matcha chocolate truffles in the middle of the storm.

"I always knew that about you, Ada. Anyone who has said differently has it backward. Jealous bitches. You'd be rich if you were a whore. You'd have your own island in the Mediterranean."

"And thus I wish I could do it."

"So you have a better conscience than most of us."

"I don't think it's my conscience. I can justify it easily enough in my head."

"Then what is it? You like to choose your lovers and not have them choose you?"

"Maybe. Yes and no. I don't really know why, exactly. I just get so angry, angry enough to want to kill someone who tries to buy me. Don't look at me like that. I'm serious."

"I don't doubt it, miss badass."

"I'm not badass. If I were, I would seduce those poor motherfuckers and make them pay. I tried once."

"Tell me."

She did not remember what she had told Kate. But now, warm and sleepless with the cars passing down below, Ada poured herself another glass of wine, lit another cigarette, and allowed herself the risk of a memory.

She did not want him. She wanted the view. The view was exquisite. The apartment was stark, white, modern, but the view sent Ada's head spinning. She could live here. She could stare out these windows day after day looking down on the city, her eyes glazing over in thought as she studied the lighted bridge. She walked over to the living room bar to make herself another gimlet. What was he doing in there? He was taking forever. No matter. Please do not come out. This time she would rather drink alone, to look out, to think. She did not like his smell. What was it? It was like a bad combination of turmeric, paprika, and stale, cancerous pheromones. Her friends would have considered him attractive, those that liked older men. Ada did not, not since Jordan.

She poured a generous four ounces of Grey Goose into her crystal glass and then added a drop more. She picked up the knife and shaved off a two-inch spiral from the lime he had left on the cutting board. Ada wrapped it around her finger, looking out at the bridge again before dropping the twist into her glass. Should she stay? Now was her chance to sneak out. Was it worth it? She felt the cowhide on the soles of her feet as she walked over to lie down on the long, low-back sofa. She sunk down into the ebony leather. What was he doing in there? The sofa was soft, a bed essentially. But did she really want it that badly? The view. The apartment. She stared at the familiar little blue box on the mirrored coffee table. She normally would have been thrilled.

"You have the most beautiful neck," he had said at dinner. "And chest."

They had sat in a booth that somehow seemed private and quiet in the packed, noisy restaurant. It was too big for two people. Ada felt

13

rather conspicuous, but she knew he was enjoying the attention. That was precisely the point. Ada thought it over the top, especially when the restaurant was so crowded, the bar three people deep, everyone dressed the way she had imagined. Ada had worn her new spiked Louboutin stilettos and a black slip dress that she knew ensured she could do anything she wanted. She had planned that far. He had not even made a reservation. Her friends were jealous when they found out where she was going, and those who had eaten there had made reservations two months in advance. Even then it was hard to get in unless you knew someone. But tonight he simply spoke to the maître d', and they walked right past the international crowd who had been waiting for their tables for over an hour. Ada felt the cold stares of the party of six whose booth they were taking. She knew he was a music executive, but really? This was how it worked. Smile, Ada.

"You comfortable?" he asked as he squeezed her knee under the table.

"Very." Ada looked up at him out of the corner of her eye.

She knew she really did not have to talk to him. She did not want to. She did not want him to know anything about her. That was easy. He just wanted to talk about himself anyway. He had the whole drive there. And now, after he had spoken to the restaurant manager who had come over, he started talking about Spain. Please stop. Why would he talk about Spain? He had it all wrong. What was he even saying? My god, he was more ignorant than she had thought. Krug and caviar. It could not distract her enough. She lifted her glass again and again, smiled at her most convincing, and then took another sip. He would have to order another bottle. Please stop talking. The server walked by. Italian maybe? Damn, he was hot. Maybe she should slip out the back.

"When were you there?" Ada asked. She could not help herself.

"Spain really is so dirty. Trash right outside my hotel room door, and no one would clean it up. No style. And a depressing lot at that. The people there just don't know how to have a good time."

"Mid- to late seventies, maybe '74 or '76, before you were born."

"Seriously? Franco died in 1975. Spain had been under a dictatorship for nearly forty years. Of course they would be depressed in '74. Not when he died though. Then it was la movida, film, fashion, language, parties! Haven't you ever seen any Almodovar movies?"

"I had no idea I was speaking to a Spanish history major."

"I'm not."

"Now you've piqued my interest. Who are you, Ada?"

The question pushed her back into herself. She was not there to teach him about Spain. She was not there to correct his seemingly never-ending babble full of mistakes and misinformation. How had he possibly become so successful with this line of thinking anyway? And she most certainly was not there to tell him who she was. For the time being she was there to smile. What else she was there to do she was not sure—or rather she was still deciding. Oscetra caviar, carpaccio of foie gras, moules au safran, black truffle tart. He motioned for the sommelier. She needed a break.

"Will you excuse me for a minute?"

"As long as it's only for a minute. I can't bear to take my eyes off of you." He grabbed her hand and squeezed it.

"Don't worry." She stared him straight in the eyes and ran her finger down his palm. "I'm fast."

His nostrils flared as he took her in, swallowing as he smiled. It was nearly unbearable. "What shall I order you for dessert?"

"Dessert can wait till later," Ada said. She slid out of the booth slowly, looked back to give him a big smile, and then felt all eyes on her as she stood up straight and focused on putting one foot in front of the other until she passed the bar to reach the ladies room.

Normally when she used that line she meant it. She did not have a sweet tooth, and sex was her favorite indulgence. Not just good nourishment but indulgent because she liked it with a fresh flare, surprising, decadent. She would rather have chocolate syrup smeared on her breasts and sucked off than to eat it over a sundae fully clothed in a restaurant booth. Ada was far more interested in having her thighs licked in the pattern of a Mayan hieroglyphic than licking creme brûlée off the spoon at the end of a meal in the finest of restaurants. Her sugar was sex—and sex alone. It always had been, and she imagined it always would be. This was precisely why this evening was not working for her.

Ada turned the lock once she was inside the large black bathroom stall. She could finally breathe now that she was alone. She set her python clutch down on the mirrored shelf. She needed to think for a moment or else consciously decide that she was not going to. She studied the chartreuse damask wallpaper that surrounded her and then put her face in her hands. Focus, Ada. What are you doing? What is the goal here? What do you want, and is it worth the price?

She knew she did not have long before she had to go back to the table. She flushed the toilet with her red sole and turned to walk out of the stall. She studied her reflection in the mirror as she walked toward the black marble sinks. Her hair was still perfect from her blowout. She did need to reapply her lipstick. It was a bold red. Ada was not playing the shrinking violet if she indeed was going to play. She still needed to get connected in the city. She needed to find a nice apartment. She needed . . .

"How much?" a woman at the sink next to her asked. Ada pulled her stare away from her own cool facade to look into the pale green eyes of the lithe brunette to her right. The woman was tall, her hair cropped short and straightened, her body tucked into her strapless leather maxi.

"About four thousand dollars," Ada said with a shrug, glancing down at her clutch. "It was a gift, so I'm not sure, exactly. It's Chanel, so you can look it up."

"No," she said as she winked at Ada. "For what's inside."

"Inside?"

"Relax. No one else is in here. I checked."

"Okay," Ada said, studying the woman's fair oval face. She dried her hands on a cloth towel. "Should I be concerned?"

"I know you weren't peeing in there."

"Really? And how do you know that?"

"I saw you come into the restaurant. Everyone did. You're fucking gorgeous, you know. Of course you do. And so am I, so we don't have to play this game."

"Agreed. But what exactly does that have to do with you following me to the toilet?"

"I followed you in here because I've been watching you, and you needed a breather from that asshole you brought," she said, stepping closer to Ada. They stood eye to eye. The woman's breath was warm. Ada noticed they were wearing the same perfume. "Don't play dumb, and don't feel bad. You don't need to pretend. I'm in the same position. I knew why you came in here, so I was listening. Of course you're smart enough to flush. Don't think I didn't notice."

"I see," Ada said. She tilted her head but did not step back. "I don't think I have what you want."

"Please. What do you want? I have cash. Take what you want. I'll pay you twice for what you paid for whatever is inside your clutch."

"Then I wish it weren't empty."

"Seriously?" the woman asked, her eyes then registering that Ada meant it. She raised her hand and put it on Ada's throat. Ada stared straight at her, and the woman smiled and bit her lip.

"Sorry," Ada whispered.

She leaned forward and kissed Ada slowly. Her lips were soft, and her breath was minty. She gripped Ada's neck tighter and kissed her harder, pulling back only when the door opened. Ada turned and left without looking behind her, touching up her lipstick with her finger as she walked back out along the bar.

When Ada got back to the table, everything had been cleared. She felt her date's stare before she locked eyes with him and slid her legs along the leather booth until she sat beside him. The was no dessert or coffee on the table, just as she had requested, and the sommelier was pouring the last of the Petrus. She felt in her stomach and did not want to drink more. Still, she did not say no to the wine. It was too good to waste. That was when she noticed the little blue box on the table. What? No. This really was exactly what she thought it was. No.

"Now tell me, Ada. What do you want to do to me?"

I want to fucking tie you up, gag you, tell you about the real Spain, and throw you backward over the Golden Gate Bridge so you can drown, she thought. *Asshole.*

Instead Ada had smiled, of course, and said some sort of nonsense that she normally would only say when she was playing around with Chris. He understood her humor and her prowess, and that was why when they fucked it was real, and it was deep. It was an equal playing field. Iron sharpening iron until they could both be sweating blood, and they still would not have stopped. Lick the blade and like it. What would Chris think of her here now, lying on this sofa with this view in her eyes? Maybe she really had loved him a little bit. Had she? It didn't matter now. This was not the place to be thinking about love. She had to be practical now, with Jordan on the Mediterranean and she in San Francisco. No more art, no more feelings, no more games, no more crazy explorations. It was time to be practical. A bitch, if that was what it took. Money was most important. If she had the money she needed, she could set herself up for life and never have to worry about anything ever again. Men would come and go; she was there to stay.

Ada sipped her vodka slowly. The view was everything—the apartment, the decor, the bar. Maybe if she were alone she could enjoy it. There was a nagging feeling that she could not shake. That is what feelings did. They ruined things that made sense. She wanted someone there with her, lying on the sofa, to be stretched out naked until the sun came up. The server, even the sommelier, maybe—but not him. Had he had a heart attack in there? She slid off the sofa and got up slowly. It was late. She should call a car. Or was he waiting for her to come in there? She walked quietly over toward the door. It stood slightly ajar. She took a deep breath and peeked inside. The bedroom was sleek, understated, colorless. There was a large platform bed covered in beige linen. To its left was a long wall of ceiling height windows. Two were open. The foot of the bed faced a limestone wall with a short rectangular fireplace carved out along the floor. A fire blazed in the dark bedroom. Light and shadows danced on the bare walls, and Ada did not move. The room smelled of tobacco and cedar. His phone vibrated on the windowsill. He was not there.

Ada wondered for moment if he had jumped out, though she could not think why. She suddenly felt scared. This was not right. Then she heard the water. She stepped inside the bedroom and walked past the fireplace. She should go home now. The phone continued to vibrate. Ada walked over to the window. The air was cold. It was foggy outside. She looked down on the windowsill and turned the phone over. The screen read, Lana. There was a photo of a long blonde stretched out on the carpet. She was naked. It was the same fireplace Ada was standing near. Ada set the phone down and saw his reflection. She put her hand over her mouth to keep from screaming. He did not see her. He was wearing a black robe and spitting out blue mouthwash into the white sink basin. He opened the door of the glass-walled shower and then dropped his robe to the floor. Water poured like a waterfall from the ceiling. He was naked. Ada blinked and turned around. No. Her heart pounded as she walked across the bedroom and back into the living room. Where were her shoes? She sat down on the sofa and put them on quickly. Her clutch would be at the door. She heard the water turn off, and she ran down the hallway.

She grabbed her clutch and slipped out the door. For the first time in her life, she felt safe inside an elevator. She did not know whether to hate or congratulate herself. She was running. She was a coward. But she now knew that she wanted more than money. She was just not sure what.

4

Ada stared at pyramids of blushing peaches before finally selecting an orange to buy, along with a kilo of cherries. She had wandered through *La Boqueria* all morning. It was a maze of colorful stalls, ripe with the ingredients of Mediterranean cuisine. Ada photographed the vast market and the hands of its vendors. She was obsessed with hands. She shot chubby brown hands full of squid, wrinkled pale hands scooping walnuts, her own freshly manicured hand against the medieval city walls not far outside. Here the selling of freshly harvested fruits of earth and sea had continued for hundreds of years. Ada embraced the tradition hungrily. She paid for the nourishment of her body to buy herself further time for the exploration of her soul. With her mesh sack filled with fruits, vegetables, nuts, and cheeses, Ada sat down on a stool to rest her legs. She slipped her camera into her soft leather tote and stared at bins of pink candy.

"Close your eyes and open your mouth."

"Is it hot?"

"Scalding … trust me, Ada. I promise it's good."

"Is this something with its head still connected? Is that why I'm closing my eyes?"

"Vegetarian."

"Oh, I'm finally having some influence on you."

"Maybe too much. Open up."

"I'm game, but no more fat today, okay?"

"Like you really need to worry about that. Last chance. It's almost gone."

She felt him gently push the fork between her lips and into her mouth. Warm, rich, salty, so simple, and yet so fucking good. Fucking good.

That's right. She was still Ada, and she was in Spain. She was alive. Ada. In Spain. It was okay, now. She would make it to twenty-one. And she was herself again, swallowing a Spanish tortilla in the middle of La Boqueria in Barcelona with a gorgeous guy who had his own apartment. When she opened her eyes, she shook her head and laughed. A wooden Pinocchio dangled above her head. Ada rubbed her own nose and smirked at Nathan before ordering a carajillo con cognac.

"Drinking in the morning now?"

"Oh, yes. I think I'm starting to feel like myself again."

Ada turned her gaze away from the pink candy to watch the passing crowd. Dangling her rope platform sandal from her toe, she stared at a woman who wore a red dress and carried a large leg of lamb. An elderly man in a white apron pulled a cart of olives and pomegranates while the young boy who held his hand gripped a bag of fish. Ada locked eyes with the large, unseeing creatures until they had passed.

She ordered an espresso but sipped it slowly, not wanting to get up again until she had decided where to spend the afternoon. Ada looked down at her hand and ran her finger over the smooth dark onyx before reaching for a cigarette to keep herself from ordering too many espressos. The bar was noisy—Catalan blending into subconscious noise as only random Spanish penetrated Ada's seemingly distant stare. She knew that she was being watched, and she easily fell into the habit of shaking her head to let a loose curl fall across her exposed temple and cheek. Ada lowered her lashes and looked left through her transparent curl. She breathed out smoke in relief when she did not recognize either of the men, her heart slowing to normal as she contemplated wearing Paulo's ring the rest of the trip to save herself trouble. She did, after all, want to prove to herself she could travel alone and remain alone.

"You are Russian?" one of the men asked.

"Nyet." Ada smiled, not wanting to go into her practiced Russian accent. "Californian."

"Better," he said. Ada stared at him. She paused to reassess her mood. He had dark hair and smelled exactly like what she wanted had he not been Spanish.

"I'm here for my father's funeral," Ada said. She stared the man in the eyes and then looked away after he did.

"I am sorry," he said.

"So am I," Ada answered. Very.

Ada loved Paulo in her way and had agreed to marry him by the end of the year. He was a good man—a catch, she constantly reminded herself. They had met when Ada photographed the wedding of Paulo's sister at a small estate in St. Helena. Ada surprised Paulo by speaking to him in Spanish and then winking at him after she had taken his picture. It was at that moment he became obsessed with her—an infatuation that somehow managed to turn itself into a muse and then love somewhere along the way. Later that first night, after too many drinks and dancing, when most of the guests had left the reception, Paulo invited Ada for a holiday at his beach house. To his surprise and her amusement, she accepted. What had started as another fling for Ada, a chance for her to play with her power over a man from Spain, had turned into something much more. Over the past two years, Ada had come to feel safe and even comfortable with Paulo, and she knew that he loved her.

Though Ada had claimed for years that she did not believe in marriage, she astonished herself earlier that year by staring into Paulo's eyes, kissing him at her most convincing, and whispering into his ear the *yes* that he had been waiting to hear. Still, the moment Ada felt the heavy ring slip onto her finger and stared down at the distracting diamond, she felt guilty, though she did not understand why. If marriage were truly inevitable, Paulo would be an ideal husband. He was stylish, sexy, rich, and he almost always let her get her way. Besides, Ada admittedly loved him with her body and a strong portion of her mind. No one, including the group closest to her, seemed to understand that Ada's heart was off-limits. Her smile and eyes masked this brilliantly.

Getting up from the bar, Ada rubbed her bare ring finger and wandered out of *La Boqueria*. Her mind played its familiar recording, and she convinced herself again through the mental lists of pros and cons that it was a good decision to marry Paulo. She was twenty-eight and tired.

Ada took a long siesta that afternoon before going out again early in the evening. She changed into a floral halter dress and took a long, slow walk up and down Las Ramblas before visiting the port. She stared out at the boats until darkness began to set in. As a group of men walked by she finally turned, glancing up at the apartment building across the street to see a light lit in the bedroom window. Ada looked down at the red polish of her toes and immediately hailed a cab.

Twenty minutes later, she sat down at a small balcony table pushed up against an iron balustrade. She changed into a floral halter dress and took a long. The cab driver had warned her as much when she asked him to stop in front of the *café cantante*, but this was precisely the type of flamenco show Ada wanted to see. There would be enough feeling in the performance to wear the mask of a moving and impassioned time, but true pain would not pierce very deep in the commercialism of it all. Ada ordered a glass of *tempranillo* and began to relax. She studied the white globe lanterns above her head before scanning the room below. The *café cantante* was mainly filled with tourists of little interest. Ada instead scrutinized the scarred wooden dance floor before finally watching the *tocaor* step up onto the stage, carrying his well-loved guitar. Ada counted its six strings and looked away to stare at her wine glass. It was nearly empty.

She did not expect the music to move her. This was not even a test. It was a game. The guitarist's first chords were raw, and Ada felt a cool breeze blow across her cheek, a pain resurfacing that she thought for one moment she recognized but then could not remember. Ada watched the *tocaor*'s fingers, long, lean, and tan. The rapidity and determination of their movements were as enigmatic and distressing as the notes that Ada's ears were drinking in. She feared the emptiness of the melodic drunkenness she would find herself in if she continued to stare. Ada determined to watch the guitarist's face instead, his dark curls held back out of his face by his ears, his faraway eyes, his lips as he licked them; and then, for some reason, he looked up in her direction. Ada surprised herself by turning away from his stare. What the fuck was wrong with her? Her embarrassment startled her.

She lifted her glass to her lips to find nothing inside and then lifted her fingers to her temple to feel along her hairline for her scar. It was little more than a pale, raised, jagged portion of skin that remained easily hidden. Lasers had done their work. When it had been a fresh wound with stitches, bright and tender, the elderly woman on the airplane told Ada that it would fade to become beautiful; that it would one day become part of her character, a battle scar of life that revealed her as a survivor, a victor. Ada remembered that at eighteen she believed the woman. She now thought her naiveté humorous. As the guitarist continued to play, Ada stood, the table shaking as she left the *café cantante* without watching the rest of the show.

5

A single flame flickered in the darkness, only shadows illuminated by its fierce glow. Silence without tranquility. The flame moved every which way, gliding, searching for the invisible wick. A voice called out. There was the clap of a solitary pair of hands, a moan, a song of unintelligible words that the flame clearly understood. She quivered. A strum, frenzied notes, the accented voice strong and beguiling. The flame twisted, spun, raised itself higher and higher, the wick finally set ablaze as she lowered herself down. The room burst into flames. Ruffles of a flamenco dress remained draped across a guitar in the center of the stage. The music intensified. Above the wooden dance floor a dove landed atop a lantern, and a black python slithered underfoot.

Ada sat up in bed to catch her breath. She wiped sweat off her forehead with the sheet and then searched for her slippers. In the kitchen she opened the large stainless steel refrigerator to choose one of the bottles of wine she had purchased at Cellar de Gelida. Her hand was unsteady as she watched the *rosado* fill her glass. It was deeper and darker than the French rosés she drank at home. Catalan was not something she had put her lips to for years, and she was beginning to remember why. Maybe it was cockiness and not intelligence that had brought her back. Maybe she should have gone to a surf camp in Nicaragua and left Spain in the blurred past. Ada walked into the living room and pulled the chaise lounge to the window to stare out into the darkness. A lone star shone above the treetops, and Ada sighed, sipping her wine as she closed her eyes and leaned her head back.

"You both know I vote for Spain," Ada said. She retied the back of her white bikini top before sitting up and climbing to her feet.

"But it'll be too hot," Sarah said. Sarah pulled her striped cover-up down over her legs. Ada shrugged. "Besides, you're the one that chose to come to Nice after Paris."

"Nice has been great, Sarah," Ash interrupted. Ada looked away, pretending to spot something down the beach as Sarah glared at her. "Barcelona's not that far, and then we could head back up north like you want."

Ada turned to watch Sarah bristle. Ash leaned back on the warm stones beside her friend, his tanned, muscular body relaxed as he looked from Sarah back up to Ada.

"Listen, you two discuss it," Ada said. She ran her toes along a stone. "I'm going for a swim."

"Hey, wait up, Ada," Ash called. "We can all talk it over and decide at dinner."

Ada opened her eyes and took another sip of the *rosado*. It was good, better than she remembered. She actually liked it. She did not want to. She put her foot up on the windowsill and felt the cool breeze on her bare skin. She wiggled her toes and stared. Ada had not seen Sarah in a decade. Ash had told Ada that Sarah got married and moved to Seattle. She had also heard through mutual friends that Sarah had just had her second baby.

"Stop it, Ash," Ada said as she felt Ash's hands run up her thighs beneath the water. A wave washed over them, and Ash pulled her legs up to wrap them around himself.

"Stop. I came out here to swim. I'm serious. You should be back with Sarah."

"Come on, Ada. How can you lie out topless and expect me not to think about last night? About tonight?"

"Not tonight. This is France, Ash. Women are free to go topless at the beach without having men grope them underwater when they want to go for a swim."

"Ada."

"No, Ash, please. Sarah's here, and besides, you got me drunk."

"Sharing a bottle or two of wine on the beach doesn't count as getting you drunk, Ada. I know you better than that."

"Well, it can't happen again. Sarah is my best friend."

"Yeah, and Chris is mine. It's not a big deal. It doesn't really change anything."

"You wouldn't be so nonchalant if Chris were still here. He might fly back after his sister's wedding, you know. And besides, since Chris and I will be at colleges on opposite coasts come fall, we've agreed to see other people. You and Sarah are still very much together. I don't want to hurt her, Ash. She loves you."

"She's insecure right now, that's all. It's not as easy to be a girl as it looks."

"Then why will she hardly let me near her? She's no fun. Look at her back there on the beach hiding under all that fabric with her face in the guidebook."

"You make it look perfectly easy, Ada," Ash said as he slipped his hand inside Ada's bikini bottom.

Ada stood up and walked back to the kitchen to pour herself another glass of wine. The clock chimed three, and she walked to the bedroom. She lit a cigarette and sat on the edge of the bed in the dark room. She promised herself once she had smoked and finished this glass she would go back to sleep.

"So what's the consensus?" Ada asked as she ripped off a piece of warm bread from the baguette and looked across the table at Sarah and Ash. Sarah would not look her in the eye. Ash smiled, but his body was tense, and Ada guessed they had been arguing before she got to the restaurant.

"I'm going to Copenhagen," Sarah said quietly.

"What do you mean, you're going to Copenhagen?" Ada asked. "You're not going alone."

"I thought sunny Spain was what you were all about, Ada," Sarah said.

"I can be Danish with the best of them," Ada joked. She normally knew how to cheer up her melancholy friend, but Sarah did not even pretend to smile. "So, are you going to check the train schedule and find a hostel for us? I did Nice."

"Yes," Sarah looked up. Her eyes locked with Ada's. "You did do Nice, didn't you, Ada?"

Dinner had not been that quiet since Chris's last night in Paris. Ada attempted to fill the void by asking Sarah dozens of questions about Denmark, kicking Ash under the table periodically to encourage him to pay attention to Sarah's overly detailed answers. A few times Sarah smiled. She even laughed when Ada attempted a Danish accent without much success. After Ada massacred the pronunciation of Tivoli she could see Sarah was pleased. Ada sighed quietly in relief and finally deemed it was safe to accept some wine from the bottle Ash had ordered. Sarah wouldn't drink any, and it seemed silly not to split it with him like normal as long as Sarah was happy.

"It'll be too cold up there to swim, probably," Ash said. He pushed his plate back and looked at Ada. Ada avoided his eyes and stared at Sarah.

"The statue of the Little Mermaid is there, isn't it, Sarah?" Ada asked.

"Mermaids are nice and all, but they aren't exactly human," Ash said.

"I mean, they can probably swim in much colder water than we can."

"It is summer, Ash, and Denmark is full of beaches where people swim, not just mermaids," Sarah said as she stood up. "Not to worry. I'm sure there are plenty of topless beaches full of girls with legs too."

Sarah backed up into the waiter and then threw open the metal gate to run down the street. Ada motioned for Ash to follow Sarah. He rolled his eyes, tossed Ada some cash, and walked down the street after Sarah. Ada stayed and finished the bottle of wine before finding her way back to the hotel alone.

Ada pulled the stark white coverlet over her head and tried to sleep. She could not. She had not thought about these things for years. In ten years she had not allowed herself to remember. They did not seem real. Could she really have been all that ten years ago? Yes. She needed to stop, stop before she got to Spain. She sat up in bed to thumb through the *Spanish Vogue* she had bought at the airport. Eighteen to twenty-eight. When she closed her eyes she was back again. How did that happen? Ada opened her eyes to read an article on skincare advances at a spa in Reykjavik and then looked through a swimsuit shoot. She studied a model, black leather one-piece, red sandals. Why Spain?

Ada knocked on the hotel door, first softly, then loudly. No answer. Sarah always carried their key. Wow, maybe she was with Ash. Wouldn't that be a surprise at night? Ash stuck his head out the door across the hall.

"You've been banished."

"What?"

"Me too."

"What are you talking about?"

"Sarah won't let me in, either. She said she had a headache and was going to bed. Come here."

"No, then I should go to bed too. That must mean we're leaving early in the morning."

"Ada." Ash held up Ada's bikini top through the door. "I told you you've been banished."

"What?" Ada walked over to the doorway to see her wet bikini bottoms drying over the chair in Ash's room. Her black backpack was on the floor. "Why is my stuff in here?"

"I didn't think you'd want it left out in the hall."

"Sarah threw my stuff out in the hall?"

Ada stepped into Ash's room. Her straw hat was on the desk next to her makeup bags and the silver cuff she had bought for herself earlier that afternoon.

"She really threw this out into the hall? What a bitch. I paid for half of that room. Someone could've stolen all of this."

"You can stay here."

"I will."

It had been dark a long time when Ada finally climbed out of bed. She slipped on a thin white tank and jean cutoffs before gathering her things into her backpack. Ash slept soundly, his flawless nude body stretched out on her side of the mattress. Ada looked down on him with a smile and shook her head. He was completely hopeless but gorgeous, and she had liked him better than she thought. She knew she wouldn't see him again for a long time, and then Chris would probably be around. Sarah was such an idiot. Ash had waited for her for so long with half their friends chasing after him. What was it with Sarah, always acting like she was smarter and better than everyone? Well, now Sarah could figure out how she'd pay for her rooms without Ada's money. Ada was going to Spain.

31

6

Ada ran down Las Ramblas, rounded the monument to Columbus, and then sprinted along Passeig de Colom. Earlier, when the sun had finally begun to rise, she still found herself wide awake, wrapped up in the white coverlet in spite of the bottle of wine she had drunk. She now attempted to regain control with a hard morning run. Ada avoided the sight of the apartment building as she passed, focusing on the port to her right instead, her sunglasses masking her tired eyes. She pushed herself forward, harder and harder, her lungs burning as her feet hit the pavement. Ada smiled as she began to sweat, her moist neck cooled by the light breeze. Her thighs stretched as she ran faster, crossing into the Parc de la Ciutadella where she could wind herself in circles along familiar pathways.

Forty minutes later, Ada finally collapsed on a bench to stretch out against the wooden slats. She took deep breaths of fresh air, focusing on releasing all her negative energy out of her body through the top of her head and back into the universe. It did not work. She concentrated on shooting everything toxic inside of her out through her feet to the core of the earth. On the third try, she still felt like shit. Then Ada remembered she had sat on this bench before. Oh, to hell with it. If she could not release her memories then she would dominate them. Fuck it all. What was it Ash always called her? A free spirit? Power broker?

The two of them still kept in touch, and he always called when he came to San Francisco. He'd bring over a bottle of Châteauneuf du Pape, they'd split a rotisserie chicken, talk a lot, and then more often than not end up in bed exhausted, after sex on the table and in the shower and on the balcony. Ash was right. Apart from Spain, Ada was a free spirit, powerful enough to pull it off and get her way. All but Spain. Ada needed to conquer Spain.

Ada stood to jog back to the hotel, stretching her arms up to the sky before taking off down the path. She slowed her pace this time as she neared the seven-story apartment building. She stopped by a palm tree to stretch her quads and stare upward into the open window. She could not see anything inside—just the sheer curtain of the living room balcony wafting back and forth in the breeze. Ada felt her scar with her fingertip and breathed in deeply with her eyes closed. Who lived there now? She toyed with the idea of finding out. What would be the harm? Maybe if a housekeeper answered, she would ask to see inside. Then she could walk around the apartment and see what had changed, herself not least of all. She could walk through the rooms one by one, allowing herself to remember a little but then in the end walk away with who she was now. Someone pulled the curtain back from the window, and Ada jumped behind the trunk of the palm tree. She peeked back up to the window and saw a man. Her fear outweighed her sense of foolishness as she sprinted back to her apartment.

Ada lit a cigarette and paced the apartment barefoot in her running shorts and sports bra. Damn it! Why had she come here? Really, what was the point? Wasn't it enough to be educated, live a life full of friends, and be at the top of her game? Ada leaned out the window to look down at the street. She ran her finger along her hairline and finished her cigarette. The woman on the plane was a liar. Scars were hell.

Ada showered and zipped up the side of her white gauze sundress. She sat down on the orange satin quilt of the bed. The cold shower had not washed away the images of the ceiling height bookcases, the hundreds of thousands of nameless pages, the squatty earthenware vase. Ada hummed to herself nervously as she stared at the dark wood of the nightstand's drawer. She stood and pretended to play the guitar, her fingers mimicking the intricate finger picking she had once loved to watch. Finally she broke into laughter. Why was she even doing this to herself? Either she was strong enough to be here, or she was not. If she wasn't, she should destroy the journal and all of her unscripted thoughts, pack her things, and spend the rest of her trip in France. But if she had managed to stop herself from throwing the journal of her mumbling self and heart over the Golden Gate Bridge countless times, or from burning it in the bathtub back at home, why should she succumb to her weakness now? Did Spain really have it in for her? That was ridiculous. Why should Barcelona have any power over her life? Look, she would even open the journal and face silly memories just to prove it.

With the brown paper crumpled up and tossed onto the floor, Ada lay down on her stomach on the bed and stared at the orange leather cover of her journal. Squeezing her eyes shut, she opened a page at random and began to read.

A doctor came just now, or at least Nathan said he was a doctor. They are friends. I thought he seemed kind of young to be an actual doctor, but I have no idea how old he is. I did not like how he looked at me. He was so serious he made me nervous. If I thought I could climb down the balcony to the street I would. I can't even get up without getting dizzy, so the balcony might as well be on the other side of the planet. Besides, they bashed my head so hard that even with the painkillers I can hardly stand it. Fucking assholes.

Nathan and the doctor did not speak Spanish to each other when they were in here, so I don't really know what they were saying. They spoke Catalan. I guess it's another romance language that they use here in Barcelona over Spanish, not that I would have been able to understand if they had spoken in Spanish, either. I tried to ask something in Spanish about the medico, and Nathan and the doctor laughed. I felt so dumb I started to cry. For some reason I couldn't help it, and now if I weren't so scared I would be totally embarrassed. I don't know what's wrong with me.

They're outside my door talking right now. I can hear them getting louder. I think they're arguing, and I'm afraid. The doctor already looked at my head and sealed it up better, but I would not let him examine me. Nathan translated everything for me when they were in here and said his friend wants me to go to the hospital. I won't go. I am bleeding a lot, but I won't go. I hate them.

What the hell was she doing here? She must be insane. No, this was not working. She had to get out of the apartment for a while. This was not okay. Ada screamed and threw the journal against the headboard. Fuck it. Then she sighed, picked up the journal from the crisp white pillow, and set it gently back into the drawer of the nightstand. She had to make it work. She would go get something to eat, wander around for a few hours, and be back to normal by evening. If not, then she could stay out late. Only that was part of the trouble. She did not want to go out alone. It did not feel right here. This was not like at home. But wasn't that the point of all this? She was strong enough. And besides, she would carry her camera with her from now on.

7

Ada took a taxi to Parc Güell. She walked through the main gate without stopping and started up the central flight of stairs. She bent low as she climbed, running her fingers along the broken white tiles of the low balustrade. On her first visit to the park, a very hot day in July, she had been so weak that she remembered stopping to sit, balancing herself on the balustrade to recover. She also remembered running her fingers along the grout in the grooves between the hundreds of pieces of broken tiles as she rested. Ada stared up at the colorful, slithering bench surrounding the Gran Placa Circular above. Nathan's voice sounded through her head. She searched for her camera in her bag.

To distract Ada from her shaky legs, Nathan had talked about Parc Güell's designer, Barcelona's famed architect Gaudí. He smiled down on her as he spoke, she straddling the balustrade. Nathan sat beside her to teach her a few words in Catalan and then gave her water from the bottle in his backpack. Ada remembered that when Nathan smiled she was always looking up at him. His smile always came down, as did his silence.

Alone this time, Ada stopped at the dragon sculpture in the center staircase. Water trickled out of the dragon's mouth. Colorful broken tiles made up the dragon's scales. Ada paused for a moment to stare before removing the lens cover of her camera.

"Smile for me, Python."

"This is Python," Nathan said, "guardian of subterranean waters."

"It looks like a dragon to me." Ada leaned in on his arm. She reached out to touch a dark blue tile along the dragon's back.

"Don't they still teach Greek mythology in high school?" Nathan asked. He took a step back, and Ada tried to balance herself on the step.

36

"Yes, and I got an A in English, thank you very much," Ada said as she turned to stare up at Nathan. "That doesn't mean I'm an expert on the guardian of subterranean waters or a python that looks like a dragon."

Nathan laughed. "Okay, okay, but it can't hurt to maybe become one. Python was born from Gaia, or Terra, you know, earth. She was the guardian of the underground waters, the earth dragon, sometimes portrayed as a dragon, sometimes as a serpent.

"An underground god? It doesn't look like a very scary dragon."

"That's because she's in Barcelona."

By the time the memory had ended, Ada was at the top of the Gran Placa Circular studying jagged pieces of mismatched tile. She clicked her camera to keep herself from touching. The longest bench in the world, a serpentine masterpiece of color, wrapped itself around the Gran Placa Circular, Python squeezing her long narrow body around Ada. The buttocks of a naked woman had formed the curvature of the seat. Ada walked to a lonely curve of Python's scales and sat. She set her camera down beside her and ran her fingers along the dirty grout beside a sea-green triangle of tile.

"Each tile has its own story," Nathan said softly, as if to himself.

"What?" Ada asked. The walk across the plaza had tired her, and she found a place to sit on the crowded bench.

"The tiles," Nathan said, looking down at her as she sat and studying her big blue eyes. "My grandma used to take me up here when I was a little boy. She told me the tiles spoke, that each had its own story to tell. We would sit down somewhere, and she would point to a tile. Then she would tell me its story. When I was older I came by myself, to see if the tiles would speak to me."

"And what did they say?"

Nathan smiled at Ada and shrugged. "Many things. There are a lot of voices surrounding us, Ada. One of the tiles is mine. Pick one to be yours."

Could she still find it? Did she want to? Where was Nathan's? He had never showed her, but she imagined it to be colorful with several sharp edges, somewhere pressed up against a black fragment, a deep blue rectangle, a sliver of orange. Ada looked up across the dirt plaza at the slew of tourists and then down at her onyx ring. She turned to stare out over Barcelona. Far in the distance was the Mediterranean Sea.

"What do you think this one says?" Ada pointed to a dark fragment shaped like the moon. Nathan reached out to trace it and then sat next to Ada in a curve of the bench.

"This one is lonely. She comes from far away."

"Being from far away isn't what makes her lonely. Home can be a bitch."

"Running doesn't get you anywhere."

"Maybe not, but it's a hell of a lot easier than staying still."

"Agreed," Nathan said. He then took Ada's finger and used it to circle the grout around a mottled yellow circle. "This is you at seven, Ada. Tell me a story."

"Ponytail, sand in my toes, grapes off the vine," Ada started as her eyes settled on the swirling shades of yellow. "I think I spent that whole summer outside. My mom told me we were going on vacation, to pack up all my favorite things in my suitcase, that she had rented a house in a vineyard so she could write. I don't think she talked to me all summer except to call my name when it got dark. She sat by the pool with her papers and typewriter, smoking and writing. She would swim naked at night under the stars. I would watch her from the open window in my satin nightgown. She was beautiful. I was scared of her. She was like another creature when she was writing. I stayed away. I spent my days running through the vineyards. I tried making raisins by putting grapes on the top of an old metal slide. I have no idea what else I did that summer. All I remember is that when it was over, we never went back home. We moved to Santa Monica. I never saw my dad again."

Nathan looked at Ada and brushed her long blonde hair out of her face. She shook her head to let the hair fall back over the stitches on her left temple. She turned her eyes away and suddenly felt self-conscious. Nathan put his hand on her knee and squeezed it.

"Okay, well, in the spirit of reciprocity, pick a tile, and I'll tell you a story," Nathan said.

Ada scanned the bench. She stood up and began to follow the serpentine curves of the bench, contemplating the myriad shapes and colors. She walked and walked. The search gave her strength. Nathan followed her without saying anything. Finally she stopped in the center on a curve. She knelt on the bench and stared out to the Mediterranean. Nathan sat down next to her. She lowered her eyes and slid her finger along the tiles in front of her, tracing her name before marking the end with a period.

"This one," Ada said.

"Black and jagged," Nathan said. He looked at Ada to gauge her expression. She looked over at him with her cool blue eyes wide open, her face blank. He swallowed. She then turned to stare out at the Mediterranean, her finger still on the tile. Nathan took a deep breath.

"This is me at twenty-two. The year between college and graduate school I decided to travel. My parents were against it. They paid for my education and thought I didn't understand what work was. To them work was money. They were good at that. We fought. They insisted I go straight to law school. No thinking, just rush through each step as fast as I could to get it all done and join the real world—one where I had a title and everything encapsulated in the single fucking stereotype they wanted."

"I thought you liked school. There's a 'Dr.' before your name on the mail. I thought that was for your doctor friend at first until I could think straight enough to realize he didn't live there."

"I like learning, Ada, and sometimes that means school, and sometimes it doesn't. I know what I need and when. At twenty-two I needed to see a bit of the world before stepping back into a classroom. There is no way I could write if I didn't have that part of my education—the dirty, real-life kind."

"What was dirty about it?"

"I lived out of a backpack for a year. My parents cut me off until I was willing to repent, move back to the States, and go to Stanford. I learned how to make my own money, which can be a very dirty experience, Ada. That's one of the reasons I brought you to my flat when I found you, and why I want you to stay until you are strong enough to go back."

Ada looked away. She bit her lip but started to cry anyway. "Fuck them."

"Do you want to talk about it?"

"Never."

"Okay." Nathan put his hand on Ada's knee and squeezed it harder. She slid her left hand down her leg and grabbed it.

"Did you go back?"

"Yes, at twenty-three, and yes, to Stanford, but not to study law."

"To write? Isn't that what you do when you're not playing the guitar?"

"Yes." Nathan laughed. "I hope I don't keep you awake."

"Sometimes. It's scary, but it excites me. I lie there in your bed and just listen. The streetlight makes the books look spooky, and I see them all caving in on me. The first nights I hid under the covers, and

I would wake up soaked with sweat. Now I can lie there naked on the sheets and feel the breeze and smell the blossoms on your balcony."

Nathan stared at Ada and swallowed. "If it keeps you up at night tell me, and I'll stop."

"I don't ever want you to stop."

Ada smiled to remember how many times she had thrown herself at Nathan. He did not want her. He was the only man she had failed at getting into bed, and she loved and hated him for it. At eighteen she cried. She would lie in his bed, running her fingers over her naked body, tracing her nipples as she listened to him play. When the bleeding finally stopped, she would open her legs and feel how wet his music made her. She would slide her fingers in and out, down and around, in rhythm with his ever-changing chords until she finally came. She would then trace his initials with her moist fingers on the pillowcase until she fell asleep.

Ada stood up. She stared out one moment longer into the faraway blue of the Mediterranean before she turned to walk back. Nathan never finished the story, or had he? She knew he had gotten his PhD and then moved into his grandmother's flat in Barcelona to research and write. His grandmother had died the year before Ada had met him. Nathan renovated the flat except for a small room upstairs where he wrote. Could he really still live there? Ada didn't think so. Nathan was too worldly and curious to stay in one place for that long. Maybe the flat was still his. But he was probably in Morocco or Havana or anywhere, really. Thank God. Ada never wanted to see him again. Ever.

8

Ada sat up in bed and caught her breath. She pushed her mess of curls out of her face and ran her fingers through her hair. Her silk nightgown was soaked through. She stripped it off and threw it to the floor. She lay back and felt the wet sheets, her body still beaded with sweat. She reached for the nightstand and felt for the box of wooden matches. She pulled herself back up onto her elbow and took a deep breath. She sat up again and felt for her slippers with her feet while lighting her cigarette. She walked naked across the room to the window. Rivulets of sweat dripped down her back as she opened the windows. She felt the night air and shivered, smoking silently as her body covered itself in goose bumps. No sleep. Pain, cold, anything. Just not sleep. Ada stared out, blowing smoke into the darkness. The other apartments were dark, shutters closed. Ada's had none—no shades, no curtains, nothing on any of the windows. Just glass, strong lines, and wrought-iron railing. Ada inhaled as she counted how many windows could see directly into her bedroom—thirty-three, thirty-four, thirty-five. She stopped counting and walked over to the bed.

Ada sat on the down comforter and lit another cigarette. She would have the apartment cleaned tomorrow and go to the pool. She could sleep during the afternoon by the water. It would be fine then. At home it was easy to sleep. Eight hours, minimum. The previous autumn she had installed blackout curtains in her apartment for those bright days when she still wanted to sleep. She loved feather beds, Belgian linen sheets, and her nightly routine when she was in her apartment alone, a luxury too rare. Ada had looked forward to sleeping in Barcelona without Paulo, to have the whole bed to herself for a month, to not have to wear an eye mask to block out his reading light, to smoke if she felt like it. Ada always slept the best in her favorite hotel in Manhattan alone. She could not go on like this here in Barcelona. Maybe she needed to sleep with someone again. Postsex sleep would do her good. No dreams to remember when she woke up, only the night before. Stop. But maybe that was what she needed, to fuck away the dreams. It always worked, but again she was unsure about Barcelona. Barcelona was a mind fuck.

"Truth or dare?"

"Dare."

Ada and Ash lay on a colorful old Berber blanket on the back lawn by the pool. It was hot, and they had swum all afternoon. Ash was home for the summer between college and graduate school. His parents were in Sweden every July, so they had the place to themselves.

"Pretend I'm that peach you're eating."

"You always turn this into a sex game."

"You always choose dare."

"Fine. Truth."

"First you have to suck me and lick my juices off your lips."

Ada bit in hard on the peach. "How about I just devour you? I like a man with bruises and teeth marks."

"Okay, fine. Let's switch it up. Truth. What is the meanest thing you've done to someone who didn't deserve it?"

"I killed a butterfly."

"What?"

"I was cruel. It was beautiful, perfect really. And I killed it. I pierced it on a big stone in Big Sur. And now it's hanging, pressed in glass in my bathroom so I can always remember that I am a murderess. Truth or dare?"

"Truth."

"Who's the last person you undressed in your thoughts?"

"You."

"Not creative."

"Then dare me to film you masturbating on the diving board."

"Pass."

"Truth or dare?"

"Truth."

"What is the scariest dream you ever had?"

"Real life is scarier than dreams. Ask a better question."

"You can't keep changing the game, Ada. And what is so scary in real life?"

"Elevators."

"Elevators?"

"Yes. How about we forget the game, and we go fuck in an elevator."

"I'm down."

9

The following morning, Ada walked up Las Ramblas, one slow, deliberate step after the other. She passed up touristy kiosks, ignored stares, and avoided eye contact until she came to a flamenco shop several blocks away. Cliché or not, flamenco haunted her. Through her dreams, she could peel back the commercialism enough to feel the raw core. Her heart pounded. She felt her blood and ran her finger over her scar. It was becoming a habit.

"Hello?" Ada looked around the empty shop. She examined the hem of a long red skirt. Its ruffles were full and layered. Ada reached for the hanger.

"¡No aquélla!" a woman's deep voice sounded over Ada's shoulder. Ada dropped her hand and turned to look down at a small woman with high cheekbones. Her gray hair was pinned up in a bun, her shoulders pushed back as she stared up into Ada's cool eyes. "¡No es para usted!"

"I'm sorry," Ada answered. The woman took the hanger and walked the skirt behind the counter. "I was just looking."

"Red not for you," the woman said. She pushed Ada to the side and picked through a rack of simple black skirts. The woman looked Ada up and down before pulling one out, a single ruffle at the bottom of the long black fabric. "This for you."

"I was only looking," Ada said. The woman thrust the skirt into her hands, and Ada felt the smooth, body-draping fabric. "I'm not a flamenco dancer. This looks like it's for practice."

"Which why is for you. You no need red, fancy *volantes.* You pretty, but body cold. You show the color when you learn dance. The color from your body, not this clothes."

"Well, I was just thinking of getting one of the traditional dresses for a costume party."

"I not sell you one."

"Why not?" Ada asked, her curiosity piqued.

"In dance you no need the color outside, the sparkle. What you need this for? You need the passion, the story in here." The woman put her hand on her stomach and breathed in deeply. Ada stared unflinchingly as the woman then reached forward and took one of Ada's wrists. She placed the other hand on Ada's chest, watching and feeling as it moved up and down. "You come tomorrow, ten o'clock."

"For the skirt?"

"For lesson. Don't be late."

"Okay, then."

Ada walked out of the shop and turned left. Where was she going? She could still feel the woman's hand on her chest. She was not in Barcelona to take flamenco lessons. She was not a gypsy. She knew how to dance, and it was different. Ada could move. She knew how to attract whatever attention she did or did not want. The last time she danced with absolute feeling ... No. Fuck that. It did not happen. Control is power. Where do you want to go? Go get a drink. The W, for Christ's sake.

A half an hour later, Ada sat down on a chaise lounge by the pool of the W and looked out to the Mediterranean. Breathe. She focused on her diaphragm and took deep, conscious breaths until her heart stopped racing. The server stood by her side and stared before bowing away quietly without speaking. "You've got this, Ada. You've got everything."

"You're holding up better than I am. You must have had five—I don't know—seven drinks since we met."

Ada looked around the studio apartment. A surfboard hung on one wall, a bike on another. A guitar was on the unmade bed. Please don't play it. The guy—what was his name?—got up and turned on the stereo. Ada felt the rhythm pulse through her. She pushed it away and lay back on the low sofa. He turned from the kitchen and looked up and down her long body. She stretched slowly, lifting her breasts and arching her back before settling back into the lull of the music. She was drunk, very drunk. That she had learned to hide this was a newly acquired talent, but she was mastering it.

"Okay, you have to go red now. No more champagne. No more chardonnay."

"I love red. Come here."

He walked over with two glasses and sat down by her hip. She sat up to take a sip—gulp, really—and then set her glass down on the wood floorboards.

"So you just got back from Europe, huh? How long did you live there? A year?"

"Not quite," Ada said. She grabbed his bicep. It was enormous. She pulled him over and down onto her. "Stop talking, please."

"You don't breathe."

"What?"

"You don't breathe. All night you've outdrunk me, outthought me, and all without breath."

"I don't know what you mean. Shhh."

"You don't want to know."

"Not really, no."

"What do you want?"

"I want you to show me how strong you are. Pick me up. I'll wrap my legs around you so you can fuck me right here in the middle of the room."

Ada looked up to see the young server standing beside her again. She smiled and lay back while looking up at him. He was tan, his head a fury of dark curls, his eyes cool and green. He handed Ada the drink menu. She took it but stared at his muscular thighs and ordered a glass of Veuve Clicquot instead without opening it. He smiled, his eyes leaving her face in favor of her chest. Her neckline was high, but her T-shirt was thin, white cotton. She gauged him by the length of his gaze. He suddenly remembered himself, and Ada watched him turn to walk around the long rectangular pool. She glanced at the red of her toes to the blue of the Mediterranean. She took another deliberate, slow breath.

"You are alone?"

A tall businessman stood beside Ada. His brown hair was slicked back to one side, and his suit was Tom Ford, but Ada could not place him by his accent.

"Happily, yes."

He sat down next to her.

"How long are you staying here?"

"As long as I feel like it."

The server arrived with Ada's champagne. The man told him to charge it to his room. He also ordered himself a Scotch. Ada scanned the Mediterranean and then paused. She took a deep breath. He was wearing one of her top three favorite colognes. She looked down into the bubbles in her glass and then took a sip. Pre-Paulo, most definitely. No vacillation. No doubt.

"You vacationing?"

"You can buy my drink, but no talking," Ada said.

She waited and could feel his gaze on her profile. He did not blink. Shit. She could do this. She always did. This was easy. Why wasn't it? She was in Barcelona to be alone. She had promised herself. Barcelona was for her only. She wasn't sharing it with anyone, even if he was six feet four, had the best teeth she had seen since she landed, and she could already feel him licking her thighs, her new Eres lingerie on the floor of his suite. Ada turned, stared directly back into his eyes, and knew it was over.

10

Ada walked up the last flight of stairs to her apartment and saw the bouquet of white roses. She opened the door and picked up the vase to read the three cursive letters of her name across a small turquoise envelope. She walked across the tiled entryway through a corridor of mirrors and into the vault-ceilinged living room. She set her bags down on the sofa before centering the bouquet on the coffee table. She lay the card down on the glass and walked into the kitchen to pour herself a glass of Priorat.

Ada leaned back against the marble counter and sighed. She finished half her glass, staring at the stainless steel pro range she had no intention of using. She finally walked back into the living room, lit a cigarette, and sat down in the chaise lounge. She inhaled and exhaled deeply, slipping off her sandals before reaching for the envelope. Paulo was so thoughtful and so generous. She wished that he had not sent these, especially today.

She was horrible. Fuck it, Ada, why? But even if she were good, damn it, she needed time to be alone in her thoughts without anyone else's interpretation of her seeping into her view. Just this once. She had a right—a right to be here to think without anyone else involved. Ada stared at the perfect white blooms and the earthenware vase as she drank the rest of the wine too quickly to enjoy it. The vase was in the shape of a bird, and it looked handmade. Ada was annoyed with how much she liked it—its beautiful curved wings, its pointed beak, the orange beak, and cream glaze.

Ada blew out smoke after lighting her second cigarette and ripped open the envelope with her fingertip. She pulled out the small white card and read, "Spain? Ada the conqueror. See you on the 4th. And bring some wine back with you. Xo—K."

What? How had Kate known? What was Paulo doing telling her friends where she was, and how did he get her address? Ada got up and walked to the bedroom, secretly happy for a reason to call back home in spite of her pounding the wall with her hand. She never should have told him where she was. He had tracked her down. Ada unlocked her suitcase and dug her phone out of her packing cubes. She dialed Kate's number before going back to the kitchen to refill her glass.

"Are you okay, Ada?"

"Of course I'm okay. Do I normally call with problems?"

"Never. I just usually don't get up at 5:00 a.m."

"Oh, sorry, Kate. I wasn't thinking. I just got the flowers you sent, and it's siesta time here. I'm drinking a nice Priorat to you."

"So, how's sunny Spain?"

"Hot! Oh, it feels so fucking good. It's like I'm melting into myself again, whatever that means. I love being somewhere hot enough to walk around the apartment naked."

"Thanks for rubbing it in. It's basically been foggy since you disappeared. We never saw the top of the Golden Gate Bridge yesterday. The sun refuses to break through."

"Well, I hate to torture you, but Barcelona is pure sunshine, riotous flowers, fresh fruit. And what beats waking up to the Mediterranean? This is real summer here, Kate."

"Okay, so who's the guy?"

"There is no guy. I'm engaged now, remember?"

"And we all love Paulo, but come on, Ada; I know you. Are you getting cold feet, or is this your own private European bachelorette party?"

"I wish. If it were, it wouldn't be here. I'm totally alone, honestly. The vase is gorgeous too though. Thank you."

"Well, if your demons really do haunt you from Barcelona, then I'm proud of you for going over there to face them off."

"What the hell are you talking about? Why would I have demons in Barcelona, and if I did, why would I be idiotic enough to come face them alone?"

"You're Ada, Ada. How should I know except that I know you well enough to know that behind that cool, controlled, classy, fucking gorgeous façade, there must be some hot, fiery Spanish demon behind it, or you wouldn't be marrying Paulo."

Ada laughed and sat back down in the chaise lounge. She stared into her glass and drank the rest in one swallow. "What a horrible thing to say! Paulo and I are good together, thank you."

"Remember when you were helping me on that travel campaign? You told me you saw San Francisco as fog and smoke, and you liked nothing better than to sweat in the cold."

"What a memory. You make me sound icy. Why are you bringing that up?"

"Because later that night you told me Nice was your favorite place on the planet; that Nice was sweat mixed with salt water, warm stones on the beach, and the sex—the place you've always gone back to with some guy or another."

"We were drunk, Kate."

"Not really, because here's what I remember most. You told me that of everywhere you've been in the world, that you'd never go back to Barcelona. You called it dirty bathroom floors, blood in the sink, stained pillowcases."

"Kate, stop."

"I've never known what that meant, Ada, and I'm not asking, but when I talked Paulo into telling me where you were, I was suddenly incredibly proud of you for facing your hell on earth."

"Thanks, but I thought I was here on vacation."

"Ada, one more thing. If you really do love Paulo and come back and still want to marry him, I'll be all smiles for you. But don't just do it because thirty is coming, and you want to try settling into the house, boat, and suburbs thing. I won't even mention babies because I already know what you'll say. You are fire, Ada, and this whole Paulo life doesn't fit you. I know he's textbook handsome and filthy rich, but he doesn't challenge you. For a life partner you need a man who will match your strength. You're too fucking passionate for Paulo, Ada, and you know it. Why else would you be in Barcelona alone?"

"Well, thanks, Kate, really. So you sent me roses so you could tell me what you really think of me?"

"Come on, Ada. How often are we totally honest? Isn't that what friends are supposed to be every once in a while? You know all your good points anyway, and if you need to hear them again I'm sure that whoever your Latin lover is waiting for you to get off the phone will be happy to tell you as soon as I hang up."

"Well, it's getting hard to concentrate with his strong hands up my dress, so I'd better go. But, Kate, thanks."

"See you back in the fog, sweetie."

11

Jetlag. It was jetlag. Simple. She would adjust any day now. Ada sat up in bed and drank water from the glass on the nightstand. She poured another from the carafe and finished that too. She slipped her silk nightgown over her naked body and walked out into the kitchen. She was breathing normally. She was in control. No nightmare this time. She opened the refrigerator and took out her leftover paella. She picked up a mussel with her fingers, felt it on her tongue, and then decided to open another bottle of local *rosat*. She carried her glass into the living room and sank down into a chair by the window. It was dark and quiet. The only light came from the streetlamp across Las Ramblas, the only sound the occasional car passing by far below.

She could do this. She was doing this. Maybe she would go to the flamenco class in the morning. Why not? Ada was back in the second bedroom with an empty glass and a lit cigarette. She would need to buy another pack in the morning. She didn't even smoke. Hadn't for years, except for in her concert days. So much for what she had told her friends about going away to a posh Icelandic resort to detox and get caught up on her sleep for a month. Should she start reading from the beginning or just open to a random page? Wait, this wasn't senior year; this was before Europe.

I am a monster. That's what Sarah says, or at least what her church said, which means it's what Sarah thinks anyway. I don't mean to be. I don't think I really am. Am I? I didn't even want to go to that camp with Sarah, but we've been friends since fourth grade, and she's invited me every summer, and I've always said no. Well, Mom hasn't let me. No religion allowed unless it's the price of a better education. You know, Catholic school … Whatever. I don't care about any of that. I was trying to be a good friend. I really was.

How is Sarah always so good? Why am I always bad? Sarah's parents won't let her come hang out over here anymore. And they sure as hell won't let me go over there. Her mom is sometimes nice, but I don't like her dad anyway. He's mean, and he has always hated me for some reason. He won't even look at me except he always stares at me when I run by their house on the beach on the weekends.

So weren't Adam and Eve supposed to be naked anyway? I didn't know Jeff would get fired or kicked out of church because of me. I tried to explain it to Sarah, but she won't even speak to me. I know it won't last long. It never does, but still. I can't tell her the truth anyway. She wouldn't get it. Plus, on top of it, my grandma won't speak to me, either. She and Sarah go to the same church, and they called me a harlot, or Jezebel, or some other weird terms like that … like I'm a seductress or witch or, oh, I know, fornicator. That was it. Maybe this vocabulary will come in handy on my text analysis on the AP literature exam. Ha! Shakespeare, Salem witch trials anyone? But it still sucks and hurts … more than I want …

My mom is furious because she said that I never should have gone to something like that, that this is what religion does to women, and I chose my own chains this time. She said I did not honor my global sisters who would give anything for the freedom I have. I don't even think she cares that I snuck out into the woods there, only the church part. I don't know. I have an extra track practice early in the morning tomorrow. I'm going to bed. I hope I dream about the new volleyball player from San Diego, Chris … yum.

Ada sighed. She slowly closed the page and slipped the journal back into the safety of the drawer. She put out her cigarette and leaned her head back against the headboard. Suddenly she was very tired. She slipped her legs under the smooth sheets and sunk her head down into the feather pillow. It was madness. So much had changed, and so much had not.

"I'll be right back," Ada had whispered to Sarah on the pew beside her.

Sarah did not even look at Ada. She kept her eyes focused ahead on the speaker. He was an old hippie, a surfer—sex, drugs, music—the whole spiel. He was in the middle of a long story about all the things he had done until he found God. Or that is what Ada assumed was coming at the end. She just did not want to wait around to hear the end of this one. There would be singing and a call forward, and she would feel Sarah so hopeful beside her, squeezing Ada's knee, praying she would get up, kneel down, and repent.

Ada walked outside into the cool mountain air. She walked up the ridge behind the main dining hall. The stars were so bright they seemed unreal. She did not really need it but she used her small flashlight and followed the familiar path past the girls' cabins. She did not feel like sleeping yet. Ada crossed the forbidden line into the cluster of boys' cabins. Everyone was in the meeting anyway. She could still hear the faint echo of the speaker's voice. Ada felt and smelled the redwoods surrounding her, so old. She felt happy. The night was getting cooler, but Ada climbed up farther until she came to a huge boulder behind the camp. She put the flashlight in her mouth and gripped the gray stone grooves with her fingers. It was not hard to climb. Once she got to the top, she turned off the flashlight. She lay back on the smooth, cool stone and studied the sky. Gorgeous.

"Hello?"

Ada heard the man's voice from the base of the boulder. Shit. Couldn't she just be alone for half an hour?

"Hello? Who's up there? Sorry, but no one is allowed out this far."

"It's me, Ada. Who are you? I just needed a little fresh air. I'll come back inside soon."

Ada heard the man start to climb. God, no. She just wanted to be alone. No more speeches. Fuck it. Couldn't she just lie here and not think about hell for five seconds? She was in heaven and intended to stay there. A flashlight shined over Ada's outstretched body. It then went dark. Who was it? Ada propped herself up on her elbows.

"What are you doing out here all alone, Ada?"

At least it was the worship leader. He was young and hot. When he played the guitar and sang, Ada just stared at him, his fingers moving up and down the neck of the guitar, his other hand strumming hard. He always wore a flannel shirt, usually gray and blue, but Ada could see his biceps through the sleeves and daydreamed about him grabbing her. Best of all, his voice was raw, and it made Ada ache. Too bad he wouldn't sing like that to me, Ada thought to herself every chapel session as the other high-schoolers sang along with their eyes closed.

"It's just that I can't sit for that long, and I don't like being inside."

He surprised Ada by sitting down next to her. Ada could smell his cologne.

"Tell me your story, Ada."

"My story?" she asked, lying back down and looking up at the stars to keep herself from kissing him.

"You know, like why did you come here? What are you looking for?"

"Oh, I didn't really come here because I'm looking for anything. I came for my friend, Sarah. She's always asked me to come, and I know it means a lot to her, this being our last summer in high school and all."

"Sarah's a sweetheart. My sister used to babysit her."

"Yes. Everyone knows Sarah is an angel."

"How come you don't ever come to church with her?"

"I go to the beach on Sundays. I don't really think you have to go to church to know God."

"Hum, really? Do you know God?"

"Maybe. I just wrote a paper about religion, about how we as different cultures create gods in our own image. It was super interesting."

"Okay. Then who is yours?"

"My god?"

"Yes."

"If I had a god, she would be absolutely gorgeous and very athletic too. She would outride, outrun, and outsmart any of the other gods. Maybe she'd even be a little scary, but not because she was mean, or harsh, or cruel. But because she was so alluring, so intelligent, so self-possessed that everyone couldn't help but worship her. She would be absolutely supreme."

Ada was so focused on what she was saying that she was surprised when she felt his hand brush across her stomach. She thought it was an accident until she looked up at him and felt him run his fingers along her abs, harder this time. She stared up into his gray eyes and did not blink. She held his gaze as she then felt his hand run up her tank top, under her bra, to cup her breast. When he started to stroke her nipple, she opened her mouth. He kissed her softly at first, but then harder, his tongue forceful and hungry within her mouth. She helped him take her bra off after he struggled, and he sucked on each breast only long enough to start unzipping her pants. Ada unzipped his, and before she knew it he was inside her, thrusting fast and hard as she gripped the stone below. He was big, and she was excited until it ended as fast as it started. He pulled out and lay back to look up at the sky next to her, and suddenly he began to cry.

12

Ada rolled over. Warm sunlight shone on her face. She felt heavy. Where was she? She opened her eyes to see her snuffed-out cigarette on the nightstand. What time was it? The street below was already noisy with traffic, and the breeze coming through the open window felt warm. Ada squinted in the sunlight. She stretched her body out long and slow under the soft, cool sheets. She yawned and stared up at the beams of the ceiling. Damn it. She had been drinking more than normal, and she could feel it. She rolled over to go back to sleep when she remembered the flamenco lesson. Seriously?

Ada dragged herself out of bed and took a quick, cool shower. She stepped out and rubbed lavender body oil slowly over her achy limbs, massaging her muscles before looking up into the mirror and into her eyes. Just go, and if you don't like it, leave. She slipped on a simple denim dress, pushed her hair back out of her eyes, and put on nude lipstick before grabbing her Hermes tote and heading for the door.

She needed to eat breakfast before she could even walk straight, let alone dance. She walked the familiar route from her apartment to La Boqueria and scanned the busy market before entering. She walked through rows of fruit stalls, bakeries, and fishmongers. She sat down briefly to sip an espresso. She really could not think. Her life was normally so regimented. This lack of planning was driving her mad.

Ada left her change on the table and searched out the stand with the ripest fruit. The vendor she chose was busy. She needed to hurry, but she could smell the apricots before she picked one up. She gently squeezed the soft, yellowish-orange skin and chose another identical to it. She selected a small bag of almonds and waited. She could not get the vendor's attention through the crowd. He was methodically handpicking several fruits and vegetables for the men in front of her. From what Ada could make out from the conversations she overheard, this was the favored produce of several local chefs.

"Ada?" A man put his large, clammy hand on Ada's arm. She looked up, and they exchanged surprised expressions. Then they both smiled.

"Mario, how are you? What are you doing here?"

"I live here now. Clara took over the restaurant back in Venice, and I opened a new eatery in the Eixample. You must come. How long are you in town?"

"For a month or so. I cannot believe you live here now. How are Clara and your daughter? She must be big by now."

"Yes, Fia is ten. She is with me this summer. She still lives with her mother in California during the school year. It's working."

"Oh, I'm sorry, Mario. I didn't realize the two of you weren't together."

"Nothing to be sorry about. Listen, you come to my place, and I'll feed you. You're as skinny as ever. We'll have a nice bottle of wine or three if I remember correctly, and we'll tell each other stories about why Barcelona."

"How can I refuse?" Ada laughed. "That time you cooked for all of us after the film festival was absolutely ridiculous. Seriously, I know you're fabulous, so yes. I'm kinda off the radar here, so I haven't been checking my phone."

"I'm at the restaurant every night. Come in anytime. You are always welcome. I'll feed you."

"Perfect. What's it called?"

"Fia, after my daughter. Little fire."

Ada kissed Mario good-bye. She left ten euros on the counter to save time and weaved her way out of the market. She bit into one of the apricots as she rushed along the sidewalk. Juice trickled down her chin. Ada took another bite, blotted her chin with her hand, and licked her lips as she kept walking. Nervous. Why? The flamenco instructor was merely a woman from the other side of the planet whom Ada had only met briefly one day ago. This was just an experiment. Like

Vegas or something. Do and disappear. If it wasn't fun or compelling, fine. It would all be over soon. Who was she kidding? What if the music was live? What if there were a guitarist in the room with them?

Ada sat in a leather bucket chair between the fireplace and the open balcony, her arms wrapped around her curled-up legs. On the right side of her face she felt the cool night air, on the left, the warmth of the flames. It was dark outside, maybe two, three in the morning. Ada did not know. She could not sleep and did not want to be alone. She had become braver over the weeks, and now when she awoke with the nightmares she followed the sound of the guitar into the living room and sat down without saying a word. Nathan glanced up briefly but then turned himself back over to the music.

Ada sat and stared. She watched his long fingers in their fury. His eyes were focused on the fire, the light reflecting off his deep-blue eyes. Ada wanted him to notice her. His mind was far away. She could tell by the way he sang. She did not understand the words. She wanted to ask, but she just sat there without moving, watching. She felt like she would cry. She shivered in the breeze, her left cheek hot from the flames. The song was passionate. When Nathan's shoulder-length hair fell into his eyes, he brushed it back, the music never interrupted. Ada wanted it to be about her. She imagined it was for a moment but could not keep up the illusion for very long. She knew that it was not. The way he sang, damn it all. It was not like the guys back home. It was not the same as the campfires on the beach or the parties at Chris's parents' house when they were in Brazil. That was easy. Ada just had to show up, have a few drinks, dance, and joke around. This was different. There were things she did not understand, and it made her feel cold.

At home she never would have been scooped up, holding her knees, trying not to cry. She would be laughing in the center of the room, handing out drinks. At home she would trust her feelings. She would climb out of the chair, crawl across the rug in front of Nathan. She would put her hands on his knees and slide her fingertips up his legs as she lifted herself into his lap. He would put his guitar down, pick her up, and then lay her down in front of the fire. She would roll over and look back as she pulled her top off over her head. Then he would not be able to keep his hands off her. She would feel him on her, in her, so deep, so hard. She would scream, and he would want to fuck her every time he saw her from then on.

But Ada was not home. There was no way she was getting up out of the chair. She did not mind being motionless as long as she could stay. There was nowhere else to go, and as alone as she felt, she knew she was somehow safe with Nathan. She did know that he noticed her sometimes. She could tell by the way he stared at her breasts when she came down to breakfast braless in a T-shirt or by the way he looked but would barely talk to her the night they went swimming at his friend's rooftop party. Ada didn't have a bathing suit so she had to borrow an Eres bikini from the host's girlfriend that was two sizes too small. He would not touch her though. He must have been in love with the girl from the song.

Ada found herself standing in front of the old black door of the flamenco studio. She placed her hand on one of the bars on the window. A chip of paint fell down onto her nude Grecian sandals. Her reflection was distorted in the mottled glass. Do not go in. Go. No. It cannot hurt you. Yes, it can. You are full of shit. It's fine. Run. Stay. You've got this. The door swung open.

"What you doing? You late."

The dancer's face was harsh. She squinted her eyes at Ada before taking her arm and pulling Ada inside. She locked the door to the shop behind them. Ada was silent. The woman's grip was unforgiving. Her fingernails dug deep into Ada's bicep. Ada bit her lip to keep from laughing. She scanned the racks of skirts as they passed. The woman was not funny. The situation was hilarious. It's a game, Ada. Play. But it's not. Stop.

"You not serious; you go home."

The woman stopped. She released Ada's arm. Ada took another step, and the woman prodded her through a dark doorway. Ada walked out into the center of the lightless room. No guitar. See. Safe. Ada lifted her head. Her slow, determined steps sounded against the floorboards. The woman stared from the doorway. Ada was motionless. The woman flipped on the light switch. The wood planks of the floor were deeply scarred. The room was still dark but for an old spotlight on Ada. The theatricality of it all added to the absurdity.

"You stay."

The woman left. The door slammed shut behind her. What the fuck? This really was hysterical. Ada noticed her reflection in the long mirror that ran the length of one of the studio walls. She looked healthy. Thin but normal anyway. She was the same. Nothing was wrong. This would be amusing. She had been young and stupid before. Now she could handle herself. Dance? Why the fuck not? Bring it on, guitar and all.

The music did not stop. Chord after chord. Song after song. They had laughed together at dinner that night. They were at the stage where the awkwardness had worn off. Nathan was no longer worried for Ada's life. Ada was comfortable enough to come out of her room and no longer blushed every time Nathan looked at her. Nathan gave Ada her first cooking lesson that night, teaching her how to grill calamari on the plancha. Fresh squid from la Bouqería, searing hot metal, olive oil, lemon.

"Careful. Give me your hand. It's hot. Yes. No. Like this. Perfect. Ah, beautiful. You have the touch, Ada. I may make you my apprentice. Now if only we could get you into wine."

"You and your wine." Ada opened the cabinet to take out two earthenware bistro plates. She set them down on the metal counter and paused. She looked back up into the cabinet and took down two

63

stemless wine glasses instead of one. She turned around to face Nathan. "Teach me."

"You're passing up rum and diet coke to please me and my culinary persuasions? Wow, you're growing up tonight, bella. Let's celebrate."

Ada would drink her first Spanish rosé. Life would be okay again. Maybe she could stay the whole year with Nathan. Maybe she could go to college in Barcelona if Nathan asked her to stay. Maybe he would even ask her to move in with him. She was already living with him, but that was different. Maybe tonight she could get him to see her for more. Maybe he was the one. Ada sat up on the counter, the metal warm on her bare legs. She handed Nathan his grandmother's old, worn corkscrew. Nathan took the rosé out of the refrigerator. The label looked like it had graffiti on it. Nathan noticed Ada staring at the spray-painted words on the bottle, and he rotated it out of view. Ada pretended not to see. She jumped down off the counter to set the table instead. Cloth napkins, sparkling water, lime. It would be okay. She was safe. Knife, fork, sea salt, no one would ever know. A small bouquet of wild roses. Nathan would never tell. The alley no longer existed. Graffiti was simply street art like before. The rosé would be good. It did not come from the city anyway. Nathan touched Ada's shoulder from behind, and she jumped. The scream came out of her mouth before she could stop it.

"You okay?"

She would not cry. God, why was she so dumb? What was wrong with her? It was nothing. Nothing happened. Nathan pulled her toward him and held her. She felt his strong body against hers. Jesus. She could hear his slow, steady heartbeat. Fuck, Ada. Hers was racing. "Pull yourself together now."

"I'm fine," Ada said. She pulled away.

"Of course you are."

"That was spacey of me. Sorry."

"No need to be. Ready for enlightenment? Let's get you into wine."

The door swung open. It banged against the brick wall. Ada blinked.

"You change now. Five minutes."

The doorknob clicked as the door closed. Ada looked to see the small pile on the floor. Leotard, skirt, shoes—all black. She picked up one of the short, stubby heels. She turned it over. There were dozens of tiny black nails pounded into the bottom. She ran her fingers over the nail heads. They were smooth and black. The shoes had never been worn. Ada needed to beat the floor, wear the paint off, make them dull and gray and then shiny and silver. Get up off your ass and work. Sink or swim. Stop pretending the stakes are so high. Stop pretending they're not. She began to undress. She folded her lace bra down the center and set it on the lone folding chair along the back wall. She draped her dress over the metal back.

"It's the color of my favorite Swatch when I was six."

"Very original. To me it's the color of just-caught Alaskan salmon, in July maybe? That bright pink that's so perfectly raw that you don't even need wasabi or tamari with your sashimi. It's that fresh."

"Okay, Mr. Writer Scholar Showoff. Or how do you prefer to be addressed? Sir Socrates? Or, no, maybe as a god? Let's just keep it real here."

"No god. Man. 'I am the wisest man alive, for I know one thing, and that is that I know nothing.'"

"I'll stick with showoff, Socrates."

"Okay, then. If you were Barbie, it would be the color of your convertible. More relatable? We all see the world differently. No right, no wrong."

"I have a Jeep, and you sound like my mom."

"That must be torturous for you."

Ada laughed. "Not really. She's actually brilliant. If you ever meet her, do not tell her I said that. The real problem is that she just doesn't really like me."

"Not possible. What's not to like?"

"Through therapy I learned that it basically comes down to that I'm not good enough. And I also like to have fun."

"That's all just a story. My story is that you are better than good, Ada. And you are the one who is brilliant. The fun part is the cherry on top. A very nice, red, juicy cherry."

She woke up naked in his bed, but not alone. This time he woke up naked beside her. The rosé was raw magic. It transformed the mangled graffiti into warm waves, salty drops of ocean on her lips. Nathan played his guitar for her, first on the terrace, then on the cool white sheets of his bedroom. The rough edges of his voice echoed through the apartment. Ada slipped her tank off over her head in the warm room, her jean shorts and panties a puddle of blue on the dark floorboards. She unhooked the black-fringed shawl from the old wooden hat stand. She danced. Freely, like a fairy that had grown up and knew her power. She felt the music. She was sound, space, time, movement. Pure energy. One with the rhythm, one with the words, the language Nathan sung was still a mystery to her. But she was a goddess in a woman's body, knowing everything and nothing as she twisted her hips and arched her back, naked but for the shawl. She raised the thin fabric high above her head, twisting, her breasts proud, her legs powerful, the shawl coming back down again as she trembled to feel its fringe tickle her skin. Every move, each intention of body, mind, and spirit, unified in some mystical conglomerate of potential meaning with Nathan's song. He began to sweat. Her chest glistened, the wetness of her skin tinged with perfume. He strummed, and she danced with such fierce primal passion that time dissolved into pure myth.

Minutes, hours, days later, both fell exhausted onto the bed. Wet. The bed a sea, soused sheets. Veins pulsating, muscles spasming. Dead, and happy anyway. And then the moment they looked at each other again, panting, chests resurrected with primal thumping, fatigue executed. Sex. Raw, hard. Biting, gripping, mouths and hands. Your everything in mine, your tongue my professor. Enlighten me. Fuck me harder. I want every piece of you. Take me. Right there. And there. Don't ever stop.

But that never happened. After the rosé, Nathan had excused himself. Ada had fallen asleep staring at the books, trying not to cry as she listened to his fiery music from the other room. And now she stood under the spotlight, waiting. Naked. The fabric of the leotard so thin it may as well have been sheer. Her nipples prominent from the front. Her back revealed shivering skin, her strong, muscular waistline taut, the bones of her shoulders jutting out. Go before it is too late. There was a rapid knock, and the door opened. Ada shook, checked herself, and stood up tall to face her instructor.

"Very good. Now you ready."

"No, actually. I'm sorry. Something just came up, and I need to leave. I will come back tomorrow."

"No."

"No?"

"Silence. Today you no talk. Your body talk. No more voice."

"What?"

"Silence!"

The woman turned on the old stereo in the corner. The room vibrated. The rhythm was steady. The recording was old. Ada felt the guitar move through her, and then she became paralyzed. No fucking way. The woman slid one foot out and began to dance, the music incarnate. She wore a long red dress, unadorned, every aspect of her body visible. She was slight and lean, her long limbs slow and controlled. Her command was unnerving, her studied oneness with rhythm of the song, the knowing look in her eye as she held Ada's gaze and then looked away. Her heels hit the floor with persuasive force. Her movements, her pace, her unrelenting stare evolved with the music—slow, miserable, fast, vexed, precise, adrenalized, yet invariably controlled and in control.

"Come."

The dance ended abruptly, the woman's sinewy arms outstretched toward the ceiling. She looked Ada up and down as she lowered her arms, her chest rising and falling as her breathing returned to normal. She placed her hands on Ada's waist and turned Ada to face their reflections in the mirror. Ada adjusted her posture to replicate her teacher—head up, shoulders back and down, chest raised, back arched. The woman turned to walk back to the stereo.

"Now you show me."

"Show you?"

"You dance."

"But you have to teach me."

"First you show me."

"No, I need a routine."

"First you dance."

The room thumped as the sound first hit the speakers. There was a rapid beat of the cajon, and then a slower rhythm. Ada lifted her chin. Her body felt the easy flow of the rhythm. This seemed familiar. She could do this. Wait. Just breathe. Hands overhead, a twist of the wrist, a stomp of her right foot. This was manageable. Pretend. There you go. Hold in your stomach. Twist. Chest up. Modern dance moves with a Spanish flair. It was polished, not raw. Pretty. Choreography was doable. It could be learned. Look how it was coming back. Feeling could be demonstrated, communicated, if not actually felt. Wasn't that meaning nowadays anyway? It was all the social intercourse really necessary. No one wanted authenticity. They said they did, but even in small doses it scared the shit out of everyone. She would master this. She could pretend right here. If she could convince the dancer that she was real, well then she had passed the test. She was back in full force.

"Stop."

"Stop? Good? Done?"

"No. This song not for you. Another."

A rapid strumming of guitar hit the studio. Fuck. Keep moving, Ada. Let it in. You've won. You dominate. Take it, control it, choke it, hold it down. Yes. Move to the right. Impeccable, sure. Rapid movements. Again. Nice. Repeat. Fire. Pain. Wait. This was real. Where was she going? No. Not acceptable. What is the choreography? Give me the fucking choreography. She stopped.

"This is not right. You need to teach me."

"You first need to discover what you want to say."

"I don't want to say anything. I just like dancing. I want people to have a good time."

"You have much to say. You very angry."

"Angry? I am not angry. This is just for fun."

"This not fun."

"No, it's not. I should go."

"You stay."

"Why did you ask me here? You don't even know me, and I clearly am not a flamenco dancer. I am on vacation and do not need any work right now."

"Estel, dance."

"Excuse me?"

"You are dance."

"What did you call me?"

"Estel."

"Don't ever call me that again. My name is Ada."

"Estel mean star."

"I know what it means. Do not call me that."

"You know what you are. What I call does not change."

"I am leaving now."

"Yes. Your time is up. Tomorrow closed. You come back day after. You take your clothes, and you be dressed and ready ten on the dot."

13

Ada walked back to her apartment without seeing anything. She forced one foot in front of the other, trying not to think or feel. She made eye contact with no one, said something passably comprehensible to the doorman, and ran up the staircase. She dropped her bag once she was inside the apartment. She took off her sandals and dress, threw them on the sofa, and walked down the hall to the bathroom. She flipped on the light switch, locked the door, and climbed up on the counter to sit on the sink basin and stare into the mirror.

She did not have her routine to distract her, to keep her running full speed ahead. Deadlines were therapy, another check off the list. Triumph. Whirlwind celebration. Back to work. In Barcelona there was nothing to check off. She felt ungrounded. There was no flow. She felt tossed about, ragged from hitting the inside of her head with jagged thoughts that would hemorrhage if she were not careful.

She was fine if she just kept going. Work. Play. Contracts. Vacation. Simple. Stress was simple. It kept her alive. Her body was strong. She was on top of everything. So fast. So easy. Even when it was not. Barcelona was different. There were no rules here. She had complete freedom, and yet she felt trapped. But by what? The past was over. She managed it all, all the time. Here she felt torture. Everywhere she looked there were memories. She was thinking. That scared her. When she was busy she did not have to face anything. It was too fast. On to the next thing. Here a simple sign could take her back, and there she was in the bathroom looking at the razor blades and remembering what it felt like to want to use one.

Fuck it, Ada; you'll be back home soon. Go for a run. Go get a drink. But she did not move. She only stared deeper into her own eyes, remembering things she did not want to know.

She had gone to the edge before. It was when she got some from Spain that first time. She had read online the easiest way to do it— the fastest, the least painful. She considered things carefully. She did not want anyone to know. She wanted it to look like an accident. No one could think they had beaten her. On those first nights, she would sit up in bed sweating, crying for hours into her pillow so her mom would not hear, sometimes not caring how they would find her body as long as she could get rid of the pain. She drew a warm bath in the tub overlooking the dark Pacific and set out the razor blade. She then poured lavender oil and sea salt under the spout, pretending she was exactly like she was before. She was not. She dipped a toe in and then melted fully into the water, not breathing, desperately trying not to feel.

She was Ada. She was kickass. She was a track star. She was a dancer. No she wasn't. She slipped herself completely under the water's edge, counting how long she could stay under before coming back up for air. Sixty-one, sixty-two, sixty-three. She almost made it two minutes once. When she came up for air, she felt her lungs, aware of each breath, her heart pounding. She looked down at her veins, pretty and blue. She asked only that if there were a god that he would murder her senses. She felt like she was being fucked deep inside with a knife—a long, sharp knife that raped her over and over again until the blood ran down her legs. And then, when she could no longer feel from the waist down, the knife would plunge into her heart. But it was not merciful. The blade would not cut her heart completely out. It just left itself in there and twisted sharply as her heart still beat, her nipples hard and cold and red. "Back under the water, Ada. Keep counting."

14

Ada wandered up and down Las Ramblas late in the day. At 8:00 p.m. it was perfectly warm. She wore a simple eyelet sundress and carried nothing but her camera and fifty euros tucked inside her thin bra. She had taken sleeping pills and was out all afternoon. It was the only way to forget that the morning had ever happened. No more fanaticism. No more Spanish nightmares. No more listening. Fresh air. Breath. Nothing more. Ada simply wanted to stretch her legs out after her siesta, and to pick up some wine and calamari before going back to her apartment to listen to old jazz and fall back asleep. Las Ramblas was a simple, convenient choice. It was crowded, distracting, and no one she could possibly know would choose to be there.

Sweat trickled down Ada's shoulder blades. Heat. Come to me. I want you. Fire. Orange. It would be over soon. What could possibly happen at this point? She would stick to her plan. Cool serenity. Maybe Paulo would get her the diamond bangles from Cartier she had been eyeing as a welcome home gift. Yes, San Francisco would be her home. Done. This experiment would be over soon, and it all would be concluded. There was nothing she really wanted to shoot on Las Ramblas. There were too many tourists, too much she had seen already. The camera was a ruse this time. It was easier to ignore comments when she pretended to photograph something. She kept her eyes upward and studied the trees through her lens or traced the edges of apartment numbers with her gaze, her camera poised as a shield. It was moderately convincing, and she was able to keep to herself for the most part. She ignored chatter, and when asked something directly, spoke in French to efficiently end most potential conversations.

"You are from Hollywood," a twenty-something man said to Ada as she wove herself through a group of nuns at the entrance of La Boqueria. "I have seen you before. I know I have. What is your name?"

His accent was French. Damn. Ada shrugged and recited a nonsensical passage in Russian she had memorized one drunken night in Saint Petersburg. She had no idea what it meant. Once she had tried it out on a Russian fling a few summers ago in San Francisco. After hearing her monologue, Sergei had picked her straight up, set her on the dresser, opened her legs, and reminded her what Saint Petersburg had felt like. She knew it must be dirty and the very best kind. It sounded like a poem. It felt like a tongue twister. This time she attempted to make it sound conversational. The creases around the man's deep hazel eyes extended as his smile got bigger. He took out his iPhone and lifted it to take a picture. Ada crossed the street.

"Russian," he said as he followed her. "I do know you, then. I have seen your work. You are a retired model."

A retired model? Worst line ever. Ada laughed to herself. Retired? If she were a model she would be. Twenty-eight and retired. Ada slipped into a flower seller's stall and considered the bouquets of sunflowers. She scanned the selection. She knew what she would find. They were all the same. This was her favorite stall though. The flowers were displayed in galvanized steel pails instead of plastic buckets. The bouquets were straightforward in their beauty, not overly done or a circus of clashing colors. At home she stopped at her corner florist after yoga on Sundays. They knew her, and her weekly bouquet was always white, from dinner plate dahlias to clean Japanese anemones, but never roses. Ever.

"I would like a dozen roses," Ada said to the florist in Spanish.

"Red, no?" he asked as he selected a bouquet without even waiting for her answer.

"No. Orange. And make that ten stems instead of a dozen."

She would buy them. She would. She had known this. Why was she doing this? She could not stop thinking about them. She might as well see them with her eyes instead of the thorny stems snagging her mind with the memories. She would rather her eyes bleed than her heart. She hated remembering she had one. The roses were a good sign. She would conquer. She paid and forced herself to hold out her arms as the florist handed her the large bouquet he had wrapped in newspaper. She carried the orange roses without looking at them, her focus straight ahead as she walked back down Las Ramblas toward the Mediterranean.

Then Ada stopped in a wine shop before she made it back to the apartment. It had become her favorite, small and cluttered but clean, and only Spanish wine. Ada kept her travel rule and only ate and drank local. She relished the daily wine lessons and stories the shop owner entertained her with.

"*Buenas, princesa*," a short, wide man said from up on a wooden ladder as Ada walked in.

"*Buenas*, Antonio." Ada walked over to the foot of the ladder and kissed him on the cheek after he came down.

"You having a party?" Antonio asked, nodding at the roses. "I have perfect wine for you."

"No, just me tonight," Ada said with a wink. "What would you recommend for a quiet night of solitude?"

"You have a quiet night of solitude?" Antonio laughed. "You don't need to be lonely, *princesa*."

"I won't be lonely with your wine. Choose something new for me to try, something I've never had before."

"Xarello."

"I like the sound of that. Is it red or white?" Ada asked. She was enjoying the conversation. She craved the distraction.

"Aromatic white. You probably drink it before in cava."

"I don't really drink cava."

"Oh, you are snob," he said, tottering his head from side to side and looking her up and down with a broad grin, "but maybe I change your mind."

Ada shrugged. "I am a bit of a snob, Antonio. I will be the first to admit it, but I am always willing to try something new, especially from you. What do you have for me?"

Antonio walked behind the counter and opened the door of a tall, narrow refrigerator. He stepped up onto a small wooden stool and stretched, reaching his hand up to the highest shelf. Antonio ran his fingertips over the foil-wrapped necks of the colorful bottles. He stopped when he felt what he was looking for, grabbing the black foil-wrapped cork with his thick fingers. He climbed down and set the wine on the glass countertop. He had chosen a green bottle with a black label and gold calligraphy, 2008 Recaredo Brut Nature Reserva.

"This is for you, my snob. From the Penedès, you know them? Thirty miles west," he said, pointing behind himself. "All biodynamic, how you like, and same method as your fancy champagne. The soil just the same as your French friends to make the sexy wine. Calcareous soil, you know it? Like your champagne. Chalky."

"I do know it." Ada smiled. "But I don't know xarello. I know chardonnay and pinot noir."

"Puff," he said with a wave of his hand. "Take this, *princesa*, and tomorrow you be a new woman—happier, wiser."

"I hope so. How much do I owe you?"

"This my gift to you."

"Antonio, please let me pay you."

"No. Beautiful woman who drink alone not pay her own drink tonight. You fall in love with this wine, and you remember who introduce you."

"I promise you that." Ada kissed him on the cheek. "Thank you."

Ada walked back to her apartment slowly, her steps reluctant, the roses tucked under one arm, her camera hung around her neck, the bottle of chilled wine in her right hand, her eyes on the distant blue. She did have the appearance of going to a party, or at the very least of celebrating something interesting. Was she? Hardly. Unless she was planning to raise her glass to survival. The fishmonger knew what Ada wanted without her having to ask. This was becoming her neighborhood fast. It could be so easy. Perfect, really. But Estel? That had to have been a mistake. Where did the dancer get off speculating and adding Ada's personal life into dancing? No. All that was so long ago. And there was no way the dancer could know. No one did. Except Chris, and he not even the truth of it, and never Estel.

"Buenas," the doorman said as he opened the door for Ada. She had reached her building. Damn. She smiled and nodded.

Sweat began to run down Ada's back again as she climbed up the spiral staircase, each flight quieter than the previous, up to her solitary doorstep. Ada set the cava down on the tile floor as she reached inside her bra for the key. Once inside, she set the roses on the kitchen counter along with the cava and went into the living room to look for her cigarettes. She removed her camera from around her neck and lay back in the chaise as she lit up. She needed to smoke at least one cigarette before she arranged the roses. She would place them on the coffee table. She would see them every time she walked through. Maybe they would die quickly. Technically they were already dead. That was the point.

"This is for you, Mommy."

Ada held up the single red rose. It had five dark crimson petals; bright yellow stamens shone out in the center. There were enough thorns to make it look wild. Ada's mom looked up from her typewriter. Ada knew she was not supposed to interrupt her when she was writing. Ada held her breath for a moment as she held out the rose. She did not want to carry it anymore.

"It looks like you," Ada said.

Her mom stared at her, her big blue eyes heavily lined in dark eyeliner. She did not speak. She caressed Ada's cheek briefly with her hand. Ada felt her cold palm for a moment. Her mom took the rose, set it on the acrylic folding writing table, and began typing again. Ada stared at her, her long fingernails fast on the keys, her clean pretty features narrowed on the text, her short haircut slicked back out of her face. She was perfect sitting there, writing with the rose. Ada was happy she had stolen it. It had made her mom happy.

Ada got up and lit her second cigarette. She opened all the windows of the apartment to feel the warm breeze on her skin. In the bedroom she took off her sandals and slipped her dress up off over her head. She walked into the bathroom and looked into the mirror. A trickle of blood ran down her inner arm. There was a smudge of red on her left breast. She moved her eyes away to turn on the faucet. Ada stepped under the downpour while the water was still cold.

"Ada, promise me one thing," her mom had said when they reached the ocean. It had taken an hour. Their cabin was far up above in the green sea of redwoods.

"What, Mommy?" Ada let go of her mom's hand after they jumped off a boulder to land in the deep sand. They had been in the forest on a writing binge all week, and both of them missed the ocean. It was too cold to swim. That did not matter. At least they could feel it, see it—blue, gray, waves, life.

"Ada, I want you to do whatever you want," her mom said.

"I want to run on the beach."

"Yes, but, Ada, listen to me." Her mom knelt down and buttoned up Ada's turquoise puffer vest as she stared her in the eyes. She pointed to Ada's chest. "What is in here?"

"My heart."

"Yes, that's your heart. Do you hear it?"

"No, not right now. I can feel it beating inside of me when I run."

"Then run. Ada, listen to me. The beating you feel when you run is your heart speaking to you. You do what makes your heart beat always, promise? You don't listen to anyone or anything else."

"Okay. Can I run now?"

"Run fast, baby."

Ada turned the faucet off and wrapped herself in a plush bath sheet. She towel-dried her hair before combing it back out of her eyes. While her body was still damp, she massaged her skin slowly and firmly with argan oil infused with jasmine. She breathed in, staring at her new tan lines in the mirror with blank eyes as she picked up a tube of Chanel lipstick. She took off the black cap, turned the red lipstick, and wrote the letters R U N across the mirror.

15

Big Sur. She went every year. It had been her favorite place as a little girl. Each November they had rented a cabin in the forest—remote, quiet, solitary. They spent Thanksgivings just the three of them—Mom, Dad, and Ada—surrounded by towering redwoods, the air crisp and clean, the long weekend wordless but for the sounds of the trees and forest floor. No one spoke. Ada learned that early on. They were there for her mom to write, for her dad to do whatever it was that he did. He was gone during the days and only came home at night to smoke his pipe. Ada and her mom normally ate alone without him after the sun had gone down. Ada's mom would grill fish or sauté scallops, put together a simple salad, and they would look up at the stars together. It was the only time during their time in Big Sur they would talk. Ada's mom would explain the constellations to Ada or teach her a new song.

The exception was Thanksgiving Day. On Thursday Ada's dad stayed in the cabin and prepared their traditional Thanksgiving meal. It was the same every year: warm spinach salad with apples and goat cheese, wild mushroom and butternut squash bread pudding, Meyer lemon cranberry sauce, and a honey-roasted fig tart for dessert. There was never any turkey. Ada did not find out that turkey was an American tradition until she was nine years old and had Thanksgiving dinner in Maine with the family of her mom's new girlfriend. Until then, Thanksgiving was the faraway Big Sur cabin, the redwoods, silence, her dad drinking Negronis all afternoon as he sliced vegetables and roasted figs.

Ada slipped on a black satin nightshirt as she walked down the hallway to the kitchen. She turned the apartment's stereo system on, and Miles Davis sounded through every room. In the kitchen, Ada tossed her journal onto the white marble counter and took out a champagne glass and an earthenware plate from the stainless steel cabinet. She chose a new white towel from the drawer. She pulled the cava out from the refrigerator, tilted the bottle to forty-five degrees, and twisted expertly. The cork was left in her right hand with only a whisper of a sigh. She tilted her glass, filled it to the brim, and took a sip. Not bad for cava. Here is to you, xarello. You may not be chardonnay, but I am not running away to France. Not tonight, anyway. Bring me your bite, your finesse. Show me what I am so afraid of.

Ada emptied the foil box of grilled calamari onto her plate and speared a piece of squid with a fork. She bit into it as she sat down on the cool barstool. Dinner was not warm anymore, but the hot chiles and fresh calamari were divine in her mouth. She looked out the large kitchen window at the dark night sky. The silhouette of an old tree blocked the view of the neighboring apartments. Ada took another sip of cava and then spun the journal around on the countertop to face her. She looked down at the cover, hesitated, and then spun it again faster. The orange corners made a jagged circle. She slammed her hand down on it to make it stop. Her grandmother had given it to her. Ada opened up to the first page to read the inscription:

Ada,

"Beauty without virtue is a flower without perfume."

Grandma

Ada turned thirteen the day she got the journal. She asked her mom why her grandma had written that.

"It's a French proverb she used to like to say to me. She wants you to have good morals, Ada. That is most important to her."

"Don't I though?"

"Ada, when Grandma looks at you, she sees your breasts and your lip gloss."

"But do you think I'm good, Mom?"

"Do good, Ada, and don't worry about if you are."

Ada was lucky her grandmother knew little about her life over the past fifteen years. Her grandmother had cut off all contact with Ada aside from Christmas cards after she had caught Ada with the neighbor boy inside her Airstream drinking tequila one summer night. Ada never would have even kept the journal except for Spain. But she had saved it, and brought it all this way to laugh at her old self. Her feelings had been real when she had written the entries, of course. But that was all dead. This was her release. She could revisit now having conquered, and then she could burn it or just simply leave it in the apartment and forget about it. Maybe she would be done with it quickly. There was still time to call her friends to meet up with her in France, and she really could have a proper bachelorette party after all.

Ada picked up the journal, her empty glass, and the bottle of cava before walking out into the living room. She poured herself another glass and settled back into the chaise lounge. Just one passage tonight, and if it went well, another tomorrow, and so forth. In no time she would be done, and she could leave. She opened up randomly, taking a sip of cava, rolling onto her side as she read the familiar penmanship.

Stacy slept here last night, and she is sleeping here again tonight. Stacy is staying the weekend with me because Mom is in Palm Springs with her new boyfriend, Steve. Stacy is Steve's daughter. She's seventeen, and Mom didn't want me spending two nights alone in the house. It was easier when Jessica lived with us. I miss Jessica, but Mom said there is no such thing as a soul mate. She said that people come in and go out of our lives at different times to teach us different things. She said I would be happiest if I didn't try to hold on to anything or anybody. I still miss Jessica though. I cried when she strapped her duffel onto her yellow Vespa to leave. Mom screamed at her, and Jessica threw the garden gnome at Mom across the front lawn. It broke the rain gutter, but even when Mom threatened to call the police, Jessica came up to the porch to give me a hug good-bye. She always used to make me green tea before school in the morning, and she would spray my pillow with lavender water every night before I went to sleep. Mom said Steve would pay for me to study abroad this summer in Paris. I don't think he wants me here.

But Stacy is perfect. She has thick, wavy hair, and she drives a red Mercedes. She took me to her tennis practice yesterday, and she will probably be the champion this year. She is so pretty. She is tall and skinny, but she has really big boobs. She let me touch them. I didn't even want to, but we went in the hot tub before her boyfriend got here last night, and she told me to feel them. She said we should go in the hot tub naked because that is how god made us and that we had nothing to be ashamed of. Stacy said that she could tell that my boobs would get as big as hers and that the best thing I could do was just love my body and enjoy it. She felt my boobs too and said that she remembered what it was like to be me. She said that everything would get much better soon.

Stacy doesn't want her dad to know that her boyfriend slept here. She said if I promised not to tell, she would take me out tonight. Her boyfriend is in a band and plays somewhere so he isn't coming. I wouldn't tell anyone anyway, but I do want to go out tonight, so I told Stacy I would keep her secret if we could go to the pier. I like the Ferris wheel at night when it's all lit up. And I like seeing all the people. I have to figure out what to wear now. I will tell you what happens tomorrow!

Ada sat up. She was amused. She had forgotten all of this. She reached over to the coffee table for her cigarettes. She lit one, took a sip of cava, and settled back down onto the chaise lounge to smoke. What had been so important to her thirteen-year-old self to record? What Ada still did remember about that weekend was that she never saw Steve or Stacy again. Ada never did find out what all the screaming was about the night they came back, but there were never any more men in the house after that.

So when we got to the pier last night, it was already dark, and there were a lot of cool people out, most of them from the high schools. I can't wait for high school! First, Stacy tried getting me into the club where her boyfriend was playing, but I don't have a fake ID yet. Stacy said I looked old for my age, but not old enough yet. She said in a few years I would be able to go anywhere I want. She is so amazing. All the guys stare at her and do anything she says. One guy bought coffee milkshakes for us, and then he won a stuffed dolphin for Stacy on the goblet toss. We ditched him by hiding in the bathroom, and then later some other guys bought our ride tickets. When they tried to get on the Ferris wheel with us, Stacy told the man that worked there that they were following us, and so he let us go on all alone. The guys started yelling at us, and then they got in a fight with the man who worked there, and I think they got thrown out. Stacy and I were laughing so hard.

Stacy asked me if I was a virgin. I was embarrassed but I told her about Jacob. He is fifteen and will get his license in the summer. I met him at the coffee shop after farmer's market a couple weekends ago with Sarah. I couldn't let Sarah see me give him my phone number so I wrote it on my cappuccino cup and left it on the table. He found it and called me. No one but Stacy knows. I showed her a picture of Jacob and me when we met up at the beach last weekend. Stacy said I should go for it. I told Stacy I wanted to, but that I was nervous. I haven't done it before, only kissing and all that.

Stacy said she would teach me. When we were on the Ferris wheel she showed me lots of things that she knew. She asked me for my rainbow unicorn lollipop. She licked it up and down and looped her tongue around it. Then she slipped it into my mouth, and I practiced. After a while she took it again and slid it way deep into her mouth and then out again. When I tried it, Stacy said that Jacob would be happy with everything I could do, but just to be sure I covered my teeth with my lips.

When we got to the top and could see out over ocean and all the lights on the shore, Stacy told me to show her how I kiss. Her mouth tasted like the lollipop, and her lips were so soft. She is perfect. It was like her lips were Claudia Schiffer's, and I could feel her huge boobs up on me. I am not a lesbian, but Stacy is a way better kisser than Jacob. And when Stacy pressed herself up against me, her boobs filled up my whole hands and felt like what I want mine to feel like. I am really not a lesbian. I do want to feel a penis up inside of me. But I also want Stacy to stay here again. I want her to teach me more tricks.

Ada tossed the journal onto the coffee table and sat up. The apartment was hot. She needed air. She opened all the windows in every room. She had wine in her mouth, sweat between her breasts. Life should be perfect. No thinking anymore. It was. It would be. She took off her satin nightshirt and threw it on the bed. She put the journal away in the bedside drawer and walked naked from room to room, smoking, pacing, convincing herself to sleep. She snuffed her cigarette out on the dish back in the kitchen, poured herself the last of the cava, and turned out the lights. She walked into the closet and slipped on a vintage nineties Dolce and Gabbana slip dress a gorgeous little bride had given her. She selected her black onyx ring, red lips, four-inch booties, and was walking up Las Ramblas before thinking again. It was nearly midnight. She needed music, a good DJ, an outdoor bar, lots of people, drinks, mindless conversation, and body heat to rival the Mediterranean breeze.

16

Ada glided through the door of the Hotel Pulitzer and headed straight up to the rooftop lounge. People were everywhere. Ada squeezed her way through the moving bodies in search of the bar. The sky was black above. Lanterns and strung-up lights made everyone look happy. The music was easy to feel, and it charged through Ada. *Gràcias.* Just a drink, and all was well. The bearded DJ smiled at Ada. She studied his tattooed arm and winked at him.

"And where did you come from?"

Ada turned and looked up at a man who smelled like a fusion of Armani Code, rum, and sex behind the locker room. He was tall, a professional athlete maybe. Basketball? His T-shirt was thin linen. He wore a gold Rolex and a beaded bracelet. Damn. She would give herself five minutes with him. She trusted herself that much.

"Lucky you. I think I just fell right out of the heavens into your lap."

He was American. Young. Dark. Cut. Must be strong as fuck.

"And what is an angel like you drinking tonight? You must be parched from your flight."

"Champagne."

"I imagined as much."

As if on cue, a curly haired server turned and handed Ada a glass of blanc de blanc. She took it. He clinked his mojito against her glass, and she shook her head at him as she stared up into his dark eyes.

"Oh, don't think I'm impressed yet." She took a sip.

"Baby, I don't even want to think with you looking like that. I just want to stare."

"What's your name?"

"Jared. Yours?"

"Jade."

"Shut up."

"What?"

He laughed. "No names, but you're not Jade."

Ada laughed. "Delilah."

"Better."

"Okay then."

He took her by the waist, and they danced. He was solid through. He could have done his workout with her sitting on top of him, blindfolded. They danced, he bought her another glass of champagne, rosé this time, and they found an empty chair to share. She offered him a cigarette. They smoked and pretended to people-watch. Mainly they eyed each other. Ada sank down deep into his lap as she listened. He was visiting friends who had an apartment down the block. He played for a team back east, first year. This was his first trip to Europe. He was going to Portugal next, but would go to Ibiza if she'd go with him.

The music got more distorted. People danced around them. Someone bummed a cigarette off Ada. Jared ordered more drinks and pulled Ada up to dance again. His hands slipped down her back. He pulled her up closer and kissed her. She didn't stop him. She kissed him back. Their drinks came. Jared sat back down in the chair, and Ada danced in front of him. She felt happy. God, she felt free. She danced with the girls next to her, and when the song ended, she fell back down into Jared's lap.

"You want to get out of here?"

"Yes."

The friends' apartment really was down the block. Ada stretched out, arched her back, and told herself not to think. Jared walked back into the bedroom with a cold bottle of rosé and two chilled glasses. They had already fucked twice, and Ada was lying on the white sheets watching the ceiling fan spin round and round in the dark room. She sat up and drank from the glass he handed to her. He then set it on the nightstand before tackling her again. He laid on top her, his body heavy, Ada motionless in surrender underneath his weight.

"So, Delilah, tell me. Do you believe in love?"

"No. Yes. No."

"Good answer."

"I don't know what love is. I don't really believe in most of it. I think when it comes down to it, it's really self against the world."

"You have to look out for yourself, for sure."

"Yes. It's not that I don't love anyone, just not really. Not like they make love out to be, anyway. I mean I want the best for my circle. I want them to like how you twist me all around into new positions I for anyone else. And how is that love, anyway? Why should I have to become someone that I'm not to please another human being?"

"Don't do it, Delilah. With that ass, you just be all you and don't put up with shit from anyone."

Ada laughed. "Seriously. I just can't embrace the whole martyrdom thing. So I am cold. I am a bitch. But actually, I am very happy when I don't care."

"You just keep on not caring all night through, then."

"Serious for one more second. Caring is what kills. Not hate. Caring tears my heart to pieces. Enough. So I don't care. Show me how much I'm going to like how you twist me all around into new positions I never knew were possible. Make me remember how flexible I am."

"Get your ass on top of me, Delilah, and you can be whatever cold bitch you want."

Ada woke up for one brief moment before dawn and realized they were lying side by side, still holding hands from the night before. She remembered. No. She did not want to. What if this was a mistake? What if it started to make her feel human again? Machine, Ada. Animal. Anything but human. She liked him. He had triggered something. Sleep. I am not eighteen. Love is never worth it. Ada still held his hand as she fell back to sleep. He rolled over and called her baby. She felt safe. Why? From what? She did not know. She did not care. She felt secure with him holding her hand, teasing her all night in spite of her mock protestations.

Later that morning she woke up alone. The covers were on the floor. She was naked on the sheets. Music played from the hallway. Had she really slept there? What time was it? Ten? Really? She rolled over onto her stomach. There was a note on the pillow next to her, the penmanship neat and precise.

You were too beautiful to wake. Don't get mad. You're gorgeous, no name. Every bit of you. Hope you find what you're looking for. You deserve it all.

She stuffed his note into her clutch, picked her dress up off the floor and slipped it back on. Where were her shoes? She turned and dropped her panties on his pillow. Damn. Why had she done this? She took a quick peek in the mirror, ran her fingers back through her hair, and opened the bedroom door. Ada smiled and waved at the young couple in the kitchen as she passed through the apartment. They offered her coffee, but she made an excuse about being late to meet her grandmother for breakfast.

Once on the street, Ada hailed a cab and was back at her apartment door in ten minutes' time. She paid the driver and turned to notice the woman on the street corner. She had seen her a dozen times. This morning it was different, even though it looked the same. The shawl over her head was leopard print. Her long skirt clashed with a gray and black cheetah pattern. The rest was black, except for a grimy turquoise bracelet. Her hands were worn with the sun. What jobs had aged them so brutally before their time? What had she done before she ended up on the sidewalk, old and dry? She had surely sucked that thumb when it was new and moist, stroked more than her fair share of penises, washed dozens of dishes, but now just held her fingers upward empty, dirty, and dry.

Her expression was authentic. The brokenness was real. This was not a scam. It was the last drop of life. Survival. No "What shoes should I wear today?" No "Do you want to try that new restaurant in the Mission or order in?" It wasn't "If I work my ass off, we can do that girls' trip to Fiji." Ada stared. The face was dark and wrinkled; her hair was pulled back into a bun streaked with gray. How old was the woman, really? The girl beside her was so young. Maybe the mother was not much older than Ada herself.

Ada was overtaken with profound sadness. Her surprise devolved into shame. It was because of the woman's station. That could easily be remedied with opportunity and generosity. It was her face. Her soul showed through on her face. No hiding. No pretending. Just bare. Naked surrender. She had given up. She sat, hands open, turned upward, eyes cast down, no will left but for survival. Ada looked away and ran upstairs. She quickly unlocked the door, threw her clutch on the entryway console, and walked straight down the hallway toward the bathroom. She flipped on the light and approached the mirror.

Her face. There were no lines. Her skin was smooth, healthy, glowing. If she was religious, it was regarding self-care, her esthetician the high priestess of her internal and external regimen. Vitamins, water, moisturizers, oils, internal, external, everything spoke of health. But was it a mask? Ada studied her eyes. Was she broken? Her eyes were cool and clear. She had fun. She still pushed the boundaries at parties, pushed her friends beyond their limits, and was more than proud of her success. But she was getting married. It was what everyone wanted, and she was horrified. The idea was still logical. It would be mutually beneficial, easy. Easy? Why was that word coming up, and when had she ever thought of marriage as something easy? Freedom was her mantra. Checking in with someone? And yet that had been easy with Paulo. He made it easy for her to focus on work. He took care of things, simplified things. She made more money now and spent less when she was with him.

And yet here she was alone in Spain. She was traveling without him before the wedding even took place. They had fought about it. It was their first fight. He thought it was out of character for her to do this. She knew that this was exactly who she was. He saw partners as talking every day. She took jobs on the East Coast so she could sleep in her own bed at Le Parker Meridian without him. And sex. Ada always wondered how she could stand up in front of her friends who knew her so well and promise fidelity for life. She was highly selective, of course, but she was unabashedly carnal.

And she knew she was not in love. Yet she had convinced herself she never would be. Therefore it really did not matter. So why was a woman on a street corner making her reconsider her decision? She believed she could be faithful to Paulo. She could. He was a surprisingly good lover, willing to learn anything and everything that pleased her. She hadn't really cheated on him either the entire time they had been together, until Spain. Ash did not count because he was an old friend, and he would not be able to stay with her anymore once she moved in with Paulo when she got back from Barcelona. It was not selling out to contribute to society by following suit in forming a social alliance that benefited … what the fuck was she saying? A social alliance?

"You are so full of shit, Ada," she said. She looked herself straight in the eyes. She laughed. She knew.

She walked back to her purse to take out twenty euros and grabbed a throw off the bed. The woman and her child would not sleep hungry or get cold come night.

17

They never went inside. Nathan did not force it. He never did. He simply walked her around the exterior, explained the Christian iconography and disputed the symbolism of the upward thrust of the eighteen towers that were meant to elevate one toward God. That was where he gave Ada the camera. The Sagrada Familia, the part gothic, part byzantine cathedral that Ada now stood in front of. She had time to walk around the Eixample before going to Mario's restaurant. Jesus. There was no way she could go inside the Sagrada Familia now. It was too massive. It felt like it was on top of her, crushing her. It weighed too much. Breathe. Fuck, it was Gaudi. It was God. It was supposed to be beautiful. Be inspired. Where is your camera? Inspired? It felt like shit. And it still was not finished.

"Добрый день."

Ada felt a hand on her bicep. She turned. "Excuse me?"

"You are Russian," a man said. He wore a steel Omega watch and a cobalt blue T-shirt.

Ada turned and looked back up at the unabashed masquerade of the cathedral. There it was. Nathan had shown her the passion facade, the skeletal Jesus outstretched on a plummeting cross.

"You are here alone?"

Ada kept walking.

"What is your name?"

"Claudia. Excuse me. You are making me late to prayer."

"It looks like a cavity."

"A cavity?"

"Yes. Like a mutant tooth."

Nathan laughed.

"Dinner later?"

Ada crossed herself and kept walking. She turned a corner and leaned up against the hard concrete. She then knew full well why she was there. It was not for Nathan. It was not to remember the moment that she had become a photographer. She came because she wanted to be punished. The realization was straightforward. She did not fight it. She wanted to feel the massive structure descend down upon her, condemn her, make her pay for her sins. She looked up at the shadowed side of the stained glass. The outside. Men in beards looked down on her. They saw. Shards of colored glass broke into a thousand pieces. They rained down on her exposed flesh. She bled, the thick droplets pooling at her feet in a puddle on the concrete floor. She felt the heat of the blood roll down her cheeks. Her chest was stained red. The pain and endless flow told her she was marred. She would scar. Her beauty was now ravished. The priest would now look her in the eye.

"Get the fuck out."

Ada walked up the block. In thirty minutes she was at Chanel. She bought herself sunglasses. Then she wandered. The Eixample neighborhood was an organized grid, the masterpiece of Catalan engineer Ildefons Cerdà. His preference for the linear saved Ada's view from the cathedral as she refused to look back. An attack of straight lines, designer shops, and tree-lined streets wasted the hours away. No getting lost, and she could walk her heart out. The hidden green of the inner courtyards of each block was out of view, like what Ada had always imagined a *riad* to be like when Nathan told her stories about Morocco. He did not like to talk about *riads* or Morocco in general, but Ada always asked him anyway.

"Are these cushions Moroccan?"

"Do they look Moroccan?"

"I don't know. I haven't been there yet. They look like what I imagine Morocco to be."

"And what is that? What does Ada imagine Morocco to be?"

"Well, mysterious. Romantic definitely. I guess, full of secrets and scents and passions."

Nathan was silent. This was the first time that Ada failed to notice when he did not answer her. Tonight she was lost in her own imagination. She conjured up images of tiled bathrooms, wrought-iron balconies, and forbidden liaisons across the Mediterranean. She knew Nathan had lived in Morocco, that he had fallen passionately in love in Tangier, that he had risked and lost all, and that his broken heart now fueled his music and poetry. At least that was the most logical story—one that Ada had invented and added details to over time. The story was fact to her, although Nathan had never told her any of these things. Was it the woman's silk robe that Ada wore each night? Was she alive? Was Nathan thinking of her right now? She was probably very beautiful, with long, full hair and striking cat eyes. She was doubtless a good lover, not just an utter cliché sex symbol like Ada, but more mysterious and earthy, with deeper knowledge of men and lovemaking. She wielded all control with but a lick of her lips.

"So you see my grandmother's old Spanish cushions as mysterious, romantic, and full of secrets and scents and passion?" Nathan rolled himself over on to his side and smirked at Ada.

Ada propped herself up for a moment, suddenly embarrassed. It was a particularly hot night, and they were lying on the rooftop, identifying what stars they could while drinking rosado and nibbling on Marcona almonds. Normally Ada was alone in bed at this time, listening in torture as Nathan played his guitar or wrote silently in his study. She felt so good to not be lying there alone, to feel Nathan's warmth beside her, to listen to his breath, to smell his cologne, to imagine he was sweating because he was thinking about her body spread out on the vibrant, quilted cushions. That if somehow she were healed, and that nothing bad had ever happened, that he would be madly in love with her, that she would forget college and move in with him for good, that he would take her to Morocco, and they would make love in their very own riad every afternoon and every night, and he would write, and she would take pictures.

"I didn't know they were your grandma's." Ada shrugged, trying to play it off. "But you never know."

Nathan laughed and rolled over onto his stomach.

"Promise me you'll never change, Ada."

"You think I'm silly."

"I think you are bewitching, but if my old, devout Catholic grandmother could hear you right now, you might be banished from the roof."

"Figures as much."

"Why do you say that?"

"Everyone good ends up hating me."

"You smack religion in the face, Ada."

"What do you mean?"

"They take one look at you, and that's enough for them to feel threatened."

"I don't know what you're talking about, but it's worth the mosquito bites being up here."

"Are you getting bitten? Let me save you. Watch."

Nathan lay down his forearm against the red cushion beside Ada. She lay there staring at his tan skin, the veins full and healthy beneath the skin, his muscle taut. She traced the contours of his arm over and over again with her eyes, imagining him touching her as he remained there perfectly still. Neither of them talked for several minutes. Ada could hear laughter from the street below. The neighborhood was quiet, but Nathan's neighbors lived well. He waited. So did she. She did not mind. He was perfect right then. A mosquito finally landed on his arm. Nathan did not flick it off or smash it. He simply flexed. The mosquito remained in his arm. He pumped his blood and flexed harder. The mosquito engorged with blood. It could not pull out. It exploded. Nathan wiped the blood off his arm and smiled at Ada. She laughed.

"You are crazy. I love it."

"I'll be your own personal mosquito net if you can bear staying out here. This heat and view are too perfect tonight to abandon for going inside."

"Can we sleep up here?"

"Why not?"

Ada's heart fluttered. She felt happy. She did not know if she ever would again, and right now she felt the familiar rush, the energy, her breasts reminding her of their presence, her thighs throbbing as she watched Nathan stretch back out again. She wanted him, yet she was content to just lie here. Other guys used the no sex, just sleeping together for the night as a line. She knew with Nathan it wasn't. She did not care. She would happily stay up there all night just to watch him sleep.

Ada sat down on a wooden bench by a palm tree at Carrer Enric Granados. She scanned the green boulevard and took out a pack of cigarettes. A vintage, mint-green Vespa pulled up off the road. A man got off with a worn messenger bag strapped across his chest. Ada watched him unstrap his leather helmet and lift it up off of his head. He was young, Spanish, a student maybe, dark wavy hair, an intentionally scruffy beard. He smiled as he walked up and sat down beside her.

"¿Rusa?"

"Nyet. Californian."

"My lucky day."

Ada handed him a cigarette. He took it. She looked in her bag for matches. He pulled out a lighter. He lit her cigarette, and they sat side-by-side, smoking in silence. Myriad people walked by. Ada studied their hands. She contemplated taking out her camera, but she sat still, smoking, feeling the warmth of the man next to her, breathing in his cologne and smoke. An old woman with dark hair and a yellow cart pulled her groceries beside her as she passed. She had been chic in her day—her Hermes scarf knotted just right, her posture perfect, her frame skeletal. Ada looked down at the man's forearm before offering him another cigarette. His tattoo was serpentine. She could not make out the words.

"What does it mean?"

"Don't look back."

"Where do you look?"

"California."

Ada laughed. "So what do you do with the memories?"

"Keep the ones I want." He lit their cigarettes. "The ones I don't never happened."

"Bravo." She turned to stare at him. "What's the most romantic thing anyone ever did for you?"

"Don't ask me to remember."

"Ha, too many to tell?"

"I don't do romantic."

"Oh, now that's some bullshit."

"It's not. What is romantic, anyway?"

"It's the language of love."

"I don't know what love is. I like presents, but calling that the language of love is a little over the top."

"Come on, California. Confess."

"Okay, Barcelona. The most romantic thing anyone did for me was save my life, right here in Spain. And he was a stranger."

"Brava. Now that is one thing this snake would look back at." He flexed his forearm. Ada touched it. He grabbed her hand.

"Okay, now you. What does that snake let you look back at?"

"When I pass my test I will remember that today beautiful California smoked with me on this bench. You are good luck."

Ada laughed. She snuffed out her cigarette and kissed him good-bye. She walked down the block until she found Mario's restaurant. She knew it before she read the stainless steel FIA inscribed in the concrete. It was like she was back in Venice Beach but with a Spanish flair. This was Abbot Kinney with old brown tile, crates of oranges, jasmine growing up over the glass facade. Ada pulled the metal door open and walked past the outdoor fire pit to the bar. The stools were old tractor seats, all occupied but one. Ada pulled it out, hung her white Birkin under the counter, and looked up at the mirrored wall of alcohol.

Vacation. This was vacation. She was warm. The sun would heal her. She could melt back into herself. The weather forecast was the same all week: days eighty-two degrees Fahrenheit, nights seventy-six. She did not even check anymore. She wore a simple, off-the-shoulder gauze minidress. This was so easy. Life really was simple. She ordered a *rosado* from the Penedès and eggs stuffed with shrimp. The bartender was brunette, pixie cut, hoop earrings, skinny. They talked a bit. Ada sat back and took a sip of the pale *rosado*. Violet and rose on the nose, strawberries in the mouth. She took the journal out of her Birkin.

Nathan just woke me up. He pushed me down on the bed and held me until I could breathe. He said I was screaming. I was having a nightmare. I feel like I just got out of the ocean. I am covered in sweat, and now Nathan is running a bath with ylang ylang salt so I can calm down and go back to sleep. The sheets are soaked through, and they smell like my lavender oil. I am so embarrassed. Nathan said that I should write the nightmare down and that he would help me understand it in the morning when I feel better. I don't want to. I don't want him to know what a mess I am.

"Happy to see you are doing well." Mario nodded toward Ada's bag. She set her journal down and winked. "It was a gift."

"I am sure it was."

"Don't go there."

"I think the last time I saw you was right after your accident. I am sorry about Zach."

"We were collaborating on a crazy project together. No one knew. Even Jordan would've been proud. Fucking bad luck. Jesus. Poor Zach. It should have been me. Zach's art, his real stuff, the stuff that made you scared of yourself, was more than I could ever understand. He was a genius."

"Thank god it wasn't you. And don't pretend you're all business now. One day when you're older you'll say, 'fuck it,' and Ms. Commercial or not, you'll show your work."

"You sound like Jordan. No Jordan tonight."

"No more scares then."

"Why did you send me orange roses?"

"What?"

"When I was in the hospital. You sent me orange roses. No one sends me orange roses except myself."

"They always make me think of you."

"What? Why?"

"I don't know. I guess, classic allure but with an edge."

"That's very sweet, but I hate them."

"Stay out of the hospital then. What happened to your arm?"

"My arm? What? Oh. I didn't realize it was all bruised."

"You've been playing rough. Enjoying yourself?"

"Ha! I think it was my flamenco teacher. She's brutal, Mario. I have to tell you all about her."

"Give me a few minutes. I'll come back."

Ada ordered marinated olives and a mushroom pizza with rosemary and olive oil. She also ordered a bottle of 1999 Vega Sicilia Unico—Castilla Leon. No more wasting time. This was her vacation. She was not eighteen, and she was not a victim. She would order the best wine, have fun, and conquer anything or anyone who crossed her. She picked the journal back up.

It was too dark to be real. I was alone. I could see my breath as I ran on the cobbled street. My lungs burned. My bare feet ached against the icy stone. I was naked except for the hooded cape I wore. The fabric was thick and rough, and I would have taken it off but for the cold. I heard wolves far away. I was more terrified of the humans. They followed me. I could not yet see their faces, but I could hear anger and laughter as they got closer. I ran faster. My feet bled. If I could get to the cathedral, I would be safe. It was the tallest building in town, and I followed my childhood footsteps through the hidden corridors of the old city and underneath the wall to the courtyard out front. I could get there. The old priest would let me in.

Only he did not.

I pounded and pounded on the front door. No one answered. I heard laughter from over the wall as my knuckles bled against the wooden door. The crowd had gotten bigger. I stepped back and looked up. I picked up a stone and threw it through the stained glass. I covered my eyes as the colored shards fell. I lifted off my cape and laid it over the windowsill to protect my skin as I climbed through. I jumped over and landed on the smooth stone of the cathedral. I tried to yank my cape free, but it was caught on the sharp fragments of glass. I left a path of blood behind me as I tiptoed through the broken pieces. I called out. There was no one.

I screamed louder. I was alone. The candelabras to my right and left were lit. Wax dripped down to the dusty floor. It smelled of must and rotted grapes. The moon shone through the stained glass. The red hid all other colors. I walked toward the altar. It was bare. The eyes of the saints looked down on me. One lifted his hand to throw his staff at my head, but the Madonna lifted her crown and crushed his skull. Blood dripped down onto my head. When I looked up, I saw that it was not the saint's blood. It was mine.

I was high on the altar, crucified. Light shone down from behind my cross. Blood dripped down my brow; my wrists were torn open—flaps of pale flesh stained with my own blood. I was naked, a spear thrust in my side. But my own martyrdom would not save me. I was slated to burn by those who would lick the crucifix blood from the parched earth. There was pounding on the door behind me. The mob was outside. They were stronger than I had been. They beat the door down. I was damned. They held torches and stones.

Whore. They called me a whore. And then I woke up.

"What are you so engrossed in?" Mario leaned up against the counter.

Ada closed the journal. She reached underneath the bar to lock it back up in her bag. "Just reading my eighteen-year-old impressions of the Sagrada Familia. I walked by the cathedral on my way here."

"Did you go inside?"

"No. Maybe if I was high. The stained glass could be fun."

"Clearly reverent."

"Mario, there are real nuns here."

"There are nuns here? Yes, Ada, nuns are real people."

Mario picked up Ada's last piece of pizza and took a bite. Ada sipped her wine and then looked over at him with a smirk.

"I can't help but stare at them whenever they pass by. I know it's rude, but I'm fascinated."

"I can imagine."

"No, really. I just can't understand. Not now."

"Not now? What? Before you were considering becoming a nun?"

"No, I mean when women had no choice. You know, marriage or the church."

"Or a courtesan, perhaps?"

"Yes. That seems better."

Mario laughed. "Yes, I can picture you now in your palace, my dear. Your sheets are the finest any man will ever find, your bed made of gold."

"Well, seriously, Mario, wouldn't that be better? Hold your breath, look the other way, not every night, of course. And I'd rather a palace be my prison than a stark cell draped in rough cloth."

"Ada, some people are very pious. They believe in another life. The earthly cell is worth the heavenly tradeoff."

"Yes, but why not have both?"

"Hell."

"Listen, Mario, really. Is being a nun necessary to escape hell? They are living hell here on earth."

"From your point of view, maybe. But they believe they are the bride of Christ. They may be happy in their devotion."

"Divine ecstasy?"

"Something like that. I don't know, Ada. I had an aunt who was a nun."

"And she was happy?"

"I don't know. She was serious and very holy, so to speak. I believe that made her happy."

"Mario, I cannot believe honestly that you are defending celibacy in any way!"

"Oh, so that's what this is about. Fucking. You stare at nuns and all you think about is fucking."

"There is more on my mind than fucking. But I'm just saying I'm sure I could get along fine without my vibrator and let my fingers do the work in that lonely bed, but no men ever?"

"Is this your plan, Ada, to get me all riled up? You absolutely know this conversation is a huge turn-on."

"Shut up. Can't you philosophize with me a little bit?"

"Not now that I'm picturing you in your cell, taking your habit off as you stare up at the lone window and reach your hand down."

"Fuck you, Mario." Ada laughed.

He squeezed her knee and got up. "Back in five."

The bartender filled Ada's glass and winked at her. Ada told her to have a glass. They agreed they wished they were drinking the bottle in bed with the guy at the other end of the bar. He was young, shaved head, impressive black beard, Japanese tattoo. They compared tasting notes, and the bartender got more pencil lead and smoke on the nose, Ada leather and incense. They agreed on the black fruit. The man to Ada's left listened and faced her when the bartender turned around. He wore ripped jeans and a vintage leather jacket.

"Your ankles."

"My ankles?"

"Yes. You have the most beautiful ankles I have ever seen."

"Excuse me?"

"Yes, I finally understand why the women used to wear long dresses to cover them up. Yours are exquisite. It makes me want to keep traveling up your leg."

"You do realize you just said that aloud."

The man tossed cash on the bar and left. Mario came out and took his barstool. The bartender slid him a Negroni. Mario clinked Ada's half-empty glass and took a sip. He nodded at her. The bartender served him bone marrow and grilled sourdough. Mario slid the plate aside and studied Ada's face.

"Okay, what, Mario?"

"Can't I look at my old friend?"

"It's rude to stare, and you are a terrible liar if you think I believe that is what you are doing."

"My little Ada, contemplating the call."

"The call?"

"You as a nun."

"Oh fuck. You're not still on that, are you?"

"My heathen friend travels halfway across the globe to contemplate the church. It is quite a surprise."

"Do you have sinful thoughts?"

"What is sinful to you?"

"Well, everything and nothing. I guess that's accurate."

"I am just having way too much fun with you, Ada. I have to go pick up Fia. Come over for dinner Friday night. I have the night off. I'll cook for you and be your therapist at the same time. We will get you through this Catholic trauma."

"Even when you are nice, you are mean, Mario. I will come to dinner though. I am not passing up your cooking. But fuck your therapy. There are better ways to get over my religion than confession."

"I thought I might enjoy the confession."

18

Ada had been following the Diamont crew in her Z4 on the bridge when the accident happened. She listened to her late-night driving playlist in a trance, focusing on the passing yellow lights of the bridge as the fog swept in. It was gorgeous. The bridge. The open road. The lights of the city. Her sound system. Her black Hervé Léger bandage dress.

It was nearly 3:00 a.m., late for San Francisco, early for Ada's French colleagues. They were ready to celebrate until dawn after having wrapped up a particularly successful collaboration on the magazine. Last call had come and gone at the bar of the St. Regis where they stayed. Jeff, an old producer from Marin, walked over to talk to Ada. He was the owner of a shoreline property in Tiburon and invited them over for an after party. Ada had been to his cliffside residence before. The trek out there would be worth it for the views of San Francisco come dawn. They could swim in the warm water pool until sunrise and then drink Bloody Marys and make breakfast burritos.

Ada loved driving the bridge at night. Her music blared. It was cold and clear. She was happy. Halloween was the last time she had been out to Jeff's place. She had woken up in a yacht as Marie Antoinette with a Swedish model who had come dressed as Adonis. He looked even more like Adonis undressed. Ada turned the music up louder. What the fuck are they doing? She slowed down as the white Land Rover swerved in front of her. Who was driving? Cut it out, asshole. Enjoy the drive. It's too perfect a night. The Land Rover scraped the center dividers. Ada braked. Then it hypercorrected and bounced off the opposite side rail. Ada braked harder and swerved. The Land Rover spun around and flipped back toward her. The sound the crash made was piercing. Fuck. Fuck, fuck, fuck. Wait.

She woke up. She was in a strange bed. It was narrow. The sheets were rough. Light flooded through the sliver of a window up above. There was a huge painting of blue splotches, like a fluffed-up, tie-dyed

T-shirt that stretched itself out and exploded. And then there was a table covered in bouquets of flowers. All of them white except one bouquet of roses in orange. What? Ada looked at her wrist. She wore a band with her name on it. What the fuck? She was in the hospital.

They released her that day. She wished they had not. She wanted painkillers, to forget. She was the one who had insisted they go to Jeff's. Zach was killed on impact, and three of her colleagues were in intensive care. Ada did not even have a scratch. They had simply hydrated her at the hospital, watched her overnight, and let her go. Three days later she went in to give blood. No one needed it anymore. It did not matter. Ada needed to do something.

Ada took off her trench coat and hung it on the hook by the door. She unwrapped her Hermes scarf from her neck and walked over to sit on the cold metal chair. She pushed up the sleeve of her black ballet sweater and stretched out her arm. Her veins bulged blue. Ada flexed and pumped her hand several times. Blood. Blue to red. Here. She did not die. This time she did not want to. "You made it. Remember what Nathan did. This is nothing."

"You have amazing veins," the phlebotomist said.

Ada did not answer. Nathan? Why had she thought of him? He did not give her blood. Yes, he did. The phlebotomist wrapped the latex tourniquet around Ada's arm. Her veins bulged like vexed serpents under her skin. No, he didn't. Ada looked away and counted down backward in French by twos. A song in Catalonian ran through her head. She blocked it out by planning out her next trip to New York. She began to run through her wardrobe, restaurant choices, and itinerary. She needed something new, more exciting. She would mix it up. Last time could not happen again.

She was bored. Why? She had always loved this. Now what would she do when she traveled? Her face remained at its most convincingly engaged as her mind wandered through various scenarios and then searched for explanations for her newfound crisis. The young actor on the barstool next to her squeezed her bare knee as he ordered her another glass of Schramsberg blanc de blanc. A third glass was Ada's inner signal that body and mind had collided enough, and that she would invite him back to her hotel room. She was usually happy at this point, feeling relaxed and playing freely with her words, letting her imagination be creative as she toyed with ideas for the night. What was wrong? This one was in his midtwenties, the face of the new Equinox ad campaign, and he was now saying naughty things to her in Italian.

Ada raised her glass, and he clinked his against hers. She swallowed a third of her sparkling wine, and he continued the conversation by telling her that her earrings reminded him of a haiku he had just read. He reached over to softly run his finger along her earlobe, tracing the diamond doves with his thumb. He ran his hand down her neck and then lightly grazed her breasts before taking a sip of his pinot noir. Ada wanted to enjoy herself. She was distracted. She still smiled at the right time, laughed when necessary, and her answers to his questions were calculated by her experience to make the rest of the night the most exciting. It had become too easy. That was it. She had conquered the game, and she was always sure of the prize.

Ada scanned the back of the bar. The myriad colorful bottles were backlit against the brick wall. Why not? It would be fun. He would be good. She could tell. And at least it would distract her from wondering why she was not into this like she normally was. Yes, this month was usually rough, but that was the point. That was why it could be the most exciting. She made sure she traveled constantly those weeks. But then she'd have to fly back in a couple days and make her pilgrimage. Maybe that was it. With that body thrust up inside her? Ada, are you crazy? This will be a good one. And yet as he pulled the candle on the table toward her and asked what she saw in it, she did not even want to play.

"Passion," Ada said as she took the last sip from her glass and stared into his deep green eyes. "I see myself reflected right back to me: hot, sweaty, an explosion of flames. But I need a wick to dance on. You?"

"You're all done."

"What?"

"You are all done. You have been sitting here fifteen minutes. If you feel okay, you may leave."

On the way out she turned to study the sack of blood. Her blood. All caught and captured. Not on the sidewalk. Not on the asphalt. Not in the elevator. Fuck them all. She walked out the door into the hallway. She was on her way to meet a longtime client for lunch to discuss an upcoming shoot in the Napa Valley. Soon she would be eating spiced carrot and cauliflower soup in Cow Hollow. Ada pushed the elevator button. And maybe a glass of Grüner Veltliner. She always took the stairs, but she was on the eighth floor and needed to go down below the building into the parking garage to get her car. Maybe she should have taken Über.

The doors to the elevator opened. Ada stepped inside to the left past two nurses and a lab technician. At least it was not too crowded. She would be in the car soon. By the time she turned her stereo on and drank some mineral water, she would be fine and on her way. Maybe she would get a massage after lunch. The elevator stopped, and one of the nurses and the lab technician stepped out. The doors closed again. The man in the center of the elevator began to pace. He was short and wore a brown sweat suit with a black leather jacket. He had a scraggly beard with the beginnings of gray streaks and smelled of coriander and freshly mowed lawn. The nurse pushed herself closer to the wall, and Ada looked away as she retied the scarf around her neck into a French knot. The man began to chant something Ada did not understand. What floor were they on?

"Dark horse!" the man shouted, startling both women. The nurse looked at Ada and then stared down at her feet. The man had stopped in front of her, six inches from her face. He stared straight at her. His skin was black, his eyes green. His focus did not waver. He chanted again, and Ada noticed two gold teeth. "You are the dark horse. The bitch of the river."

"What the fuck?" Ada did not move. She watched the man's hands carefully. She thought he might pull out a knife.

"Beware!"

The nurse pushed the elevator buttons.

"Beware of the dark whore. The dark-horse bitch."

The man waved his hands in front of himself in a circular motion. He stared at Ada as he made various signs to protect himself. Ada's heart pounded. She was trapped against the elevator wall. She could not breathe. Her scarf was choking her, but she did not take her eyes off the man. Her stare excited and disturbed him. He jolted back and forth as if to avert her. She did not move. She was afraid. Her fear made her angry.

"The great whore. The dark-horse bitch of the water's edge. Beware."
The elevator stopped. The nurse stepped out. The man blocked Ada in. The doors were closing.

"You will not triumph, dark-horse bitch."

Jesus Christ. He was going to attack her. And then he collapsed. He started to spasm. Was he having a seizure? The elevator doors opened, and Ada jumped over his body. She ran to her car and never looked back.

19

Sleep had finally come to Ada in the very last stages of night before the light of dawn. And she slept. Ten hours, eleven? It did not matter. When she awoke, she just lay there in the bed looking up at the ceiling, stretching her body out long under the blanket, yawning as she massaged her arms and legs with her hands. The sheets were not soaked beneath her. If the nightmares had come, she did not remember. Her stomach growled. She pulled herself up out of bed to make coffee and *pa amb tomàquet.*

In the kitchen, she grilled the sourdough bread from the restaurant. She sliced and mashed Mario's vine-ripened tomatoes. Ada poured and sipped hot, black coffee as she rubbed her toast with freshly grated garlic, smashed the sweet, juicy tomatoes on top, and then drizzled pale green olive oil over it all. She ate like she was starving, poring over a metro schedule and drinking her coffee as she planned the route of her lazy day.

By the time she was dressed in her denim romper, had pulled her hair up in a ponytail and tucked a new biography of Catherine the Great into her favorite old leather Alaïa tote, it was her normal siesta time. She grabbed the key off the dining room table and forced herself out the door and down the long, winding staircase before she could change her mind. If she opened a bottle of rosé and lay down to read in the chaise near the breezy front window now, a nap would ensue. The whole day would be gone, and she would be up all night. Ada reached street level and said hello to the doorman. He asked if she was walking today or would like him to hail her a taxi. She fought the urge to say yes, smiled as she told him she was walking, and followed her plan. She had finally slept. She would stay true to form—the form of her girlhood. Today was going to be a play day—nothing serious, nothing too much in character. No work, no sex, no thinking—just good, old-fashioned childlike fun. It was much easier to pretend, and to distance herself from work and relationships without a phone. It was as liberating as it was torturous. Ada would be in the moment today, nothing else.

Stepping down into the metro station triggered the first of the queasiness. People stared. A group of young men surrounded her and filled her head with their calls and whistles. She was determined. She stared at her gladiator sandals as she placed one foot after another down the concrete stairs. She would descend. A businessman made no secret of looking her up and down. She would not notice. This was fun—like being eighteen, like not having a care except to live in the moment and then choose where she wanted to go next. Ada wanted to feel that again. She was clutching her tote tight. She had forgotten that real freedom existed. Was it naïveté or innocence? Those days of waking up, stretching out in bed, and asking herself, "What should I do today?"

Ada listened to a man play the guitar on the platform. He was too good to be performing down there. Ada wanted to block it out. It was too perfect, haunting. At eighteen she would have given him money. At twenty-eight she just stood there staring at the tracks, not making eye contact with anyone who looked at her, her mind set in a blaze of disparate thoughts. She did not live her life in fear, did she? No. Look at all she had become. Look at her now stepping onto the metro. She faced her fear like this over and over. Conquerer. It was bullshit, but it worked. The fear had become so normal that she for the most part forgot it was there, like breath—or rather, the lack thereof. She reminded herself several times throughout the day to keep breathing. Was she still running? At home her system of coping mechanisms was painfully fine-tuned. It really did work. Why go back to the scene of the crime? She did not need to be a hero. Why face it? It was because, more than anything else, Ada wanted to remember what it was like to not be afraid. Even now, she used her mind to overpower her heart. She could push it back, not play through the scenes of the buying countless metro tickets, country after country, until she reached Spain alone. The first time Nathan had taken her out, after she had spent a month in bed, she froze when they reached the metro steps down the block from his apartment. Nathan did not force her. He did not even encourage her to take the plunge. He simply had taken her by the hand and walked her down the sidewalk to the park. They sat on a park bench and watched the birds fight over crumbs. They did not speak. They did not have to.

Ada found a seat and gripped her tote in her lap. She looked at her hands folded in her lap, distracted herself from the stares by her smooth, familiar onyx. Beside her, a man wearing large headphones stared at his phone, his backpack between his feet on the floor. A woman with cheap turquoise sandals beside her read a novel in Portuguese. The man seated on the opposite side of her wore a camel-hued cardigan and smelled of old sweat. She had done it. She was on the metro and on her way. The train stopped at the next station. The doors opened. A man stepped on with an accordion. He smiled directly at Ada. He was missing his top front tooth, and there was an oddly large gold tooth next to the gap. The train started again. The man greeted everyone in Italian and began to play. Ada had to move her legs at an angle to keep from touching his stained trousers. The accordion opened and closed right in front of her face. There was no escaping the music. Ada felt as though she was in a carnival.

"I want to play!" Ada ran over to the counter and picked up the toy rifle. She knew she could hit one of those floating balloons. She would aim for the yellow one first. If she had enough bullets, she would hit the blue one afterward to win a teddy bear for Sarah as well.

"The last thing you need is another stuffed animal."

"Please, Daddy."

"Ada, you won't win anyway. They rig these things. Don't you see? They make it so it looks easy, but you can't win. It's a money trap. Look. See how even though that man is aiming straight ahead, the pellet goes to the right, and the balloons float away."

"But it's fun."

113

"How is it fun to pay to shoot a pretend gun at floating balloons?"

"I might win, Daddy."

"Fine. Here's five dollars. Play, and I'll meet you at the car."

The train stopped at the next metro station. Ada stepped past the man with the accordion. She climbed up the stairs and then scanned the sunny street, stretching her legs as she walked to her next stop. She would take the tram and spend the rest of the day at Parc d'Atraccions Tidibabo, the old, turn-of-the-century amusement park overlooking Barcelona in the hills above the Mediterranean. The views from above the city were breathtaking. Ada took out her camera and focused on Barcelona down below. She laughed. She could not stop finding angles that intrigued her. She was mad about the city—its square blocks, its curves, the Mediterranean blue that outlined it all. Seeing it from up above. Is this what love felt like? She had come for the views—Barcelona spread out below her, the blue sea as far as she could stare into the distance, the feeling of safety that looking down provoked in her. Why hadn't Nathan ever brought her here?

"You're very pretty."

Ada turned to look down at a young boy. He stared straight back up at Ada. She smirked.

"Why, aren't you sweet," Ada said. She put her hand on her chest and studied his big blue eyes and freckled nose. "How old are you?"

"Six," he said. "Do you want to sit by me?"

Ada looked over to see his parents. They were sharing a large double scoop of green ice cream. The mother pulled a waffle wafer out of the center of the sweating cup. She scooped up a large bite of ice cream and placed it in the father's mouth. Green dripped down his chin. They glanced over at Ada, and she smiled. They smiled back. Their six-year-old son took Ada's hand and pulled her toward Avió, a red airplane that jutted out high above Barcelona below.

"I need to buy a ticket," Ada said. She could get some great shots of city from up so high. The boy would not let go of her hand.

"I have a ticket for you," he said. The boy pushed his sandy curls out of his eyes and stuck his hand in his pocket. He wore plaid cargo shorts, a faded polo, and canvas sneakers. "This ride is very historical."

"Oh, really?"

"Yes. It is the world's first flight simulator. It opened in 1928. No one got to go on airplanes back then. That is why it's so special."

"Is it now? Well, thank you for inviting me on."

"The plane is a replica of the first flight between Barcelona and Madrid."

"Very impressive. I like a man who knows his geography."

"And history?"

"Absolutely. Even better."

The boy's parents had sat down on a bench to watch. Ada stopped listening to the boy as they waited in line for the old plane. Could she be a mother? Would she wake up and make breakfast for the boy? Then what? Lay out his jeans and sweater on his solar system comforter, pack his lunch with organic edamame salad, and then walk him to school down a tree-lined street? Ada looked at the father's shoes to assess what she might then be doing the rest of the day. Kensington? Would she be like her friends: errands, charities, salons, and then kids to piano, lacrosse, swimming? Oh, and dinner, of course. She would need to plan that, or coordinate with the nanny/chef. Bedtime stories too. What about sex? Was that scheduled? If it was not spontaneous, then who initiated? Was that part of the checklist? Maybe that was why the ice cream his parents shared seemed more erotic than innocent.

"Why are you scared?"

115

"What? I'm not scared."

"Yes, you are. You keep putting your hand in your purse and then taking it out with nothing there."

"I was just thinking about taking pictures, that's all. I'm a photographer."

"Someone should take a picture of you."

"Let's take one together."

"Do you have a boyfriend?"

"No," Ada answered.

"Well, you'd better start thinking about that," Andrew said.

"Oh, really? I once had a boyfriend in high school named Andrew. Maybe I'll wait for you to grow up."

"That will be a long time."

"I'm in no rush."

They prepared to board. It was like getting in an old train in the sky. Ada looked back at the parents as Andrew talked about a movie Ada had never heard of. They looked as though they were making decisions, planning something, definitely not on a holiday in the middle of summer. Is that what she and Paulo looked like? Please, God, no. She should feel guilty. She did not. And that was the only reason she ever felt guilty: for not feeling guilty.

The sun was so hot. It felt like heaven. Drops of sweat gathered between Ada's breasts and ran down her stomach, puddling in her belly button. She wore a cherry tomato Eres bathing suit. The neckline plunged clear down to her navel, the waistband a shade darker with her steady sweat. She lay beside the pool at the Andaz at Wailea, Paulo beside her. Ada read a new bestselling biography on Robert Mapplethorpe while Paulo worked on his laptop. He had the perfect tan, a little hair on his chest, and Ada's favorite—very defined abs. He wore short navy Armani swim trunks and stroked his beard constantly in thought, except for when the server came by. Then he would stop to order Ada another glass of champagne and himself a beer. They had been lying there for an hour, at least. Ada was just about to doze off when Paulo snapped his laptop closed. He lay down and stretched back on his chaise lounge before he rolled over to stare at Ada. She smiled and put her book down.

"I love you, Ada," he said. It just came out. He was completely relaxed.

"What?" Ada said. She panicked. Paulo's words hung in the air. She did not know what to do with them. From the look on his face there was nothing she needed to do. This was always the part where she felt like she was sinking. She was usually prepared for it and had already packed her bag and sent it with the bellboy down to the car. This time it took her by surprise. She needed to regain control fast. "What's not to love in a place like this, gorgeous?"

"The place isn't what I'm thinking about. I love you, Ada."

"How? Why?" The words slipped out. As soon as she said them she began to strategize. How could she manage to keep their travel together fun and nothing else? They had only just met a few months ago. Love had not even crossed her mind.

"I have not seen anyone else since that evening we met."

Fuck. She slipped over onto her stomach. She needed a second. This confession scared her more. Where did she go from here?

"I know we never talked about that," Paulo continued, "but it was my choice. I just haven't wanted to spend time with anyone else."

Okay fine, but love?

"I don't want to scare you off, Ada. You are the most breathtaking woman I have ever met."

There it was.

117

"I could not imagine being here with anyone but you," Paulo concluded.

Ada reached her hand over and squeezed Paulo's thigh.

"Let's enjoy paradise together, then. Shall we?" she said. "You have no idea how much I love being here with you."

Ada slowly ran her finger higher up his thigh and then up under his swim trunks. She tilted her head in the direction of their suite and winked.

The ride was over. Ada's camera had stayed in her bag. This was enough fun. Ada said good-bye to the boy and walked the city until midnight.

20

Darkness. So black. The occasional passing car. Quiet. Solitary. Ada held the journal in her hands but did not move. She just sat there. Staring. There was nothing. Perfection. To breathe with nothing. A light flickered across the way. A man pulled the drapes back from the open window. He was nude and well hung. He lit a cigarette. This was the first neighbor Ada had seen. Grateful. No friends, no conversations, just nothing. She had no idea who any of them were, the inhabitants of the silent flats that surrounded her, or what their lives were like—if they lived in Barcelona or if these were second homes. The man smoked quickly. Inhale and enjoy, buddy. He lit another cigarette. The man leaned over the railing and flicked his ashes down to the street far below.

His hair was bleached blond. He was pale, skinny. A tattoo covered the length of his left arm. A woman's hand reached around from behind the curtain. She grabbed the cigarette from his mouth. He slapped her, hard, and took it back. Ada pulled away from the window. The man had grabbed the woman and wrapped her arms behind her back. He held them with one hand. He bent her over the railing of the window. Her breasts swung as she struggled to free herself. He continued to smoke. The woman turned her head to bite him. He moved from side to side, smoking, holding, dodging, laughing. He finally spit the cigarette out the window and pulled her up, pushing her against the window frame. She kissed him.

Ada went to bed. She lit a cigarette and opened the journal.

Jordan made me do it. It was my idea. He does not even know. But he made me. I would not have been brave enough, otherwise. It is stupid, I know. No one will even see the photographs. Why did he push that hard? He provoked me to create, to actually give birth. Fuck him. There is no real bravery in what I did. But it fucking scared me to the core. I could not stop shaking. When Jordan got home, he asked me what was wrong. I was in a blanket in the hammock, shaking. I had already done the shoot, but I told him I hadn't. I don't remember even going out there. I don't even remember taking the pictures. He found them. He showed me. He made me do it. They are not real. I will destroy them. They are not real.

Jesus. Was she that insane when she was pursuing her art with him? Maybe commercialism was not a sellout after all. Maybe it was mental health in all its carnality. If she was a sellout, she was a living one. Crude money was real money. Weddings were her Babylon. If she was a whore now, at least she was good at it.

Piles of wedding dresses covered the ivory coverlet of the king-size bed in the Mandarin Oriental Hotel. Ada had flown out to New York City with the bride. She would shoot the wine country wedding in October, but she was asked to play stylist as well. Brides had started to request that she fly out with them to choose their look for their big day—the look Ada would capture, and they could cherish through better or worse. Lace, pearls, backless, pink floral—even a pastel tartan. This bride could not decide. Long, short, straight, full. Jesus. Rein her in, Ada. Brides. She had learned what to say. How to make them feel the full power of their beauty on that day. Ada always smiled. This one would be happy with her photos postwedding. She was beautiful. Ada just needed to help her see herself through a new lens.

Ada's phone rang. It was Kate. Ada told the bride to put on the strapless lavender gown and excused herself. She answered the phone in the hallway and walked back to her room to look out at Central Park.

"Hey, love. You miss me?"

"No, I was glad to have you gone this morning."

"What? At boot camp? Don't tell me you've found a more kickass girlfriend. Did you cheat on me at the juice bar afterward?"

"No. I wouldn't do wheatgrass shots with anyone but you, Ada. I just had to get to the new instructor before you got back."

"Ah, fuck. What is he like?"

"Hands off. Did you read your mom's new piece?"

"The one in the anthology? No. She just sent it to me. I put it in my bag to read on the plane on the way back."

"It's about you."

"About me?"

"Yes. It's good."

"It's always good. But about me? Really? She hasn't called me since Thanksgiving."

"Read it and call me when you're done working. There's someone I want you to meet from the gallery tonight."

Ada did not want to read it. She had given up on her mother years ago. She still loved her, was proud of her—always would be. But a relationship? No. Ada rummaged through her crocodile tote. She found the anthology and walked over to the chaise and lay down. She looked down forty floors to the treetops below. She sighed and began to read.

Her locks were golden like her father's. She was a child born out of an archaic illustration. Brothers Grimm, chubby cheeks, big blue eyes, "Look, Mommy!" her constant refrain. I had a heart after all. This child was mine. I had never meant her to be. Fairy-tale looks? Fairy-tale life? Princess was not a word that had been part of my vocabulary growing up. I was the dark, slight beauty of a braless age, she the curvy heroine of the land of plenty. I screamed in protest, refused compromise. She licked honey off her lips and met her friends at the mall after school. I had sewn my own clothes. Design. Earth. And yet I was the one who gave Ada her own credit card. Fashion. Power. I had slept on the sand under the stars. Mushrooms, connection, touch. She slept on boats with men whose names she could not remember. Coke, domination, cameras.

Horrible mother, you say. Ignorance is bliss. Is it? You tell me. This fairy-tale baby was mine, no one else's. I did not want her, and yet she was mine. Living, breathing flesh. Goddess incarnate. An angel to this unbeliever. I could not be my own mother. I would not fill her head with stories of the dark forest, make her fear the woodsman, face the orphanage alone, or become the servant in a house that belonged to her. I gave her the gift I had never been given. Freedom. Absolute freedom. I told her to listen to her own heart, to tell anyone who told her differently to fuck off, even if that voice was my own, and I was the one being sworn at.

I protected Ada by setting her free. She would not live in my mother's fortress, not feel the tied wrists of my own childhood. She would roam, wander, learn, and her fairy tale would come true, even if I did not believe in childhood myths.

Today is March 17, the birthday of my daughter, the death day of my mother. The line bears no resemblance, and yet the two are intrinsically linked, a connection that would not connect other than for the very reason it is connected. In me. Perhaps the only thing my daughter and mother would agree on is this: I am a failure. And yet I am the glue. I am woman. A believer. A heathen. A lover. A murderer. An intellectual. A fool. A victim. A warrior. Blood and marrow. Flesh and breath. I am infinite. And so are our daughters. They just do not know it yet.

Ada tossed the anthology to the floor. She took a deep breath and stood up. She went back to the bride's room to invite her to dinner. The bride opened the door. Her face was flushed from crying.

"Are you okay?" Ada asked.

"Yes, thank you!" The bride put her arms around Ada and squeezed. Ada held her for a couple of seconds and then pulled away.

"I came to see if you wanted to eat at the bar downstairs."

"No, but thank you. I was so afraid before this trip. I didn't want to be the fat, dieting bride, and, well, a failure. Finding the dress is supposed to be something fun, something you do with your mom and girlfriends, something like a fairy-tale ending. But I couldn't do it, Ada. I am so glad I found you. This dress you chose, it's so unconventional, but, well, I feel like I can be the bride in it, and not everyone will be staring at my bridesmaids instead."

"Fuck anything different. You are beautiful. And don't let anyone ever make you think differently."

"And I know you'll take the most amazing pictures and make me look skinny, even with all the lace."

"I promise." Ada smiled. "Tell me one thing. Why do you love him?"

"Tony? He's my soul mate."

"Oh. You are very lucky. And you look like a perfect dream." Ada squeezed the bride's hand and winked. "Sweet dreams."

Ada turned and walked down the hallway. She remembered what Jordan had said before he had died.

"Why do I feel like I was with you long ago in another place? Like you were a goddess, and I was your god, and we reigned together somewhere far away? It sounds so cheesy, I know, Ada. But then, I know that it is true. No one can convince me otherwise. When I touch you, I touch the eternal. I touch the divine. Stop laughing. I know these things. You know them too."

That was Jordan though. He was no soul mate. Just a soul and a mate. They all were. Down to the bar with you, my love. You are dining alone tonight.

21

Ada walked through the front door of the studio five minutes before the hour. She had woken with the sun, run seven miles, stretched an hour to her old Paris playlist, and breakfasted on espresso and poached eggs. Her flamenco teacher talked to another student in the shop but motioned for Ada to go in and ready herself. As Ada slipped into the simple black leotard and long skirt, she prepared herself by not preparing herself. Why was she there? It did not matter. She was.

The dancer stepped into the doorway. She stared at Ada. Ada lifted her chest, pulled her shoulders back, her abdomen in, her feet firm against the bruised floor. She stared at her reflection and tried not to blink. Her chest filled with air. She forced her breathing downward. Fuck, she could not remember it all. So she steadied herself in her eyes. "You can, and you will, Ada. Don't break." The dancer came and stood beside her. She was half Ada's size.

"What is this?" She placed her cold finger between Ada's shoulder blades.

"My spine," Ada said. She did not flinch. She faced forward in the mirror, her breathing shallow.

"Yes, your spine. Your posture. You reach up. Vertical."

"Yes. And that is good, right?"

"Horizontal."

"Horizontal?"

"You are raised up. Beautiful posture to walk Las Ramblas. But to dance you need horizontal."

"What do you mean?"

"Crucifixion."

"Excuse me?"

"Your body is a cross. You stretch up. Now you must stretch across."

She pressed between Ada's shoulder blades. Ada pushed her chest out farther. Her shoulders fell back into place.

"Do not move. Stay."

She walked out. The door clicked shut behind her. Ada was alone in the room. She tried to breathe naturally. She felt false, her posture so confident she did not believe herself. She waited. She studied her face. She liked this lipstick. She needed new earrings. Paulo had given these to her. They were Chanel. They were beautiful, really, but she did not feel elegant anymore. She felt displaced, frazzled, holding her pose while wishing she could dance wild on the beach in big gold hoops.

"Congratulations, Ada."

Ada's mom and her mom's girlfriend, Carrie, had come home from Thailand to be at Ada's high school graduation. They took her out to their favorite neighborhood sushi restaurant after the ceremony. Carrie quizzed Ada on all the parties she would go to that night. She told Ada that she could wear her red Hervé Léger bandage dress. Ada's mom gave her taxi money and told her to spend the night at Chris's if she wanted to.

"We got something for you," Carrie said.

"I thought the trip to Europe was my graduation present."

"Give it to her," Carrie told Ada's mom.

"We both thought of you when we saw these, Ada."

Ada's mom handed her a small box. Ada slipped off the ribbon. Inside were hoop earrings made of python ribs.

"What did you see?"

Ada gasped. She did not realize her teacher was back. She tried to regain her composure.

126

"I was just focused on keeping the position."

"No. What did you see?"

"I tried to stay focused. I just had a brief memory of the past. It was nothing."

"It was everything."

"What?"

"You want the future, no?"

"Yes."

"Then you are a crucifix. Keep your chest exposed. Your heart open to the future. You see the past, and you let your shoulders fall, then you live in terror. No, not you. You are hanging on a cross. To release the trauma in yourself and your audience, you open and die."

"Die?"

"You afraid?"

"Yes."

"That's because you don't believe in resurrection."

"Well, how about you teach me some moves? I think that would be easier."

"Easy is a waste of time."

"I appreciate the symbolism, really, but I don't like to associate dancing with dying."

"Try again."

"Try what?"

"I go. You hold this pose. You are crucified."

She left again. What the fuck? Ada stared back into her eyes. They were glossy. This was ridiculous. What was she supposed to do here? A raised chest was sexy; being nailed to a cross was macabre. Surely dance did not need to be that dramatic. Vulnerable, fine. She could tap into old emotions to add to the allure, and for the sake of believability with the audience. But expose her body to her traumatic past and lift it up as an offering of rebirth? Dance was dance. Fun, sex, release. Easy.

"You smell like summer."

"It is summer."

"Jasmine."

Breath. Sweat. Teeth. A gold crucifix. Pain.

"Wait. What are you doing? Don't touch me like that. I don't even know you. Get the fuck off of me."

"Will you show me?" Ada asked.

"Come back!" Ada shouted to the dancer from the abandoned room. The door opened. The dancer stepped back inside. Ada pushed her shoulders back and down. She lifted her chest again. She slowed her breathing. She was ready now. She waited for the dancer to reach her.

She nodded once, pivoted, and turned on the stereo. The room thudded. The song ached betrayal. Ada pressed herself against the bar of the back wall of the studio. The bulb overhead flickered. The dancer was poised. She was still. Her eyes narrowed on something far away. Now her gestures were dramatic, controlled, all-commanding, ethereal. She moved around an invisible target. Her movements were calculated yet fluid. Her feet were sharp and sure. Her arms floated as if parting water. The voice of the recording ached. He was gone. Her face grimaced. Her arms twisted. Her fingers mastered the space. Her body writhed in torment. Beauty incarnate. Her face hardened, and then cracked into a nostalgic illusion that spoke of a complicated past, a bloodbath of the heart. Loss. It was all that it came down to. Passion, anger, revenge were but for what? Loss.

The dancer seduced the space, rejected it, stomped it to death and then surrendered herself to the heavens. She had won and lost. Her chest lifted up and down forcefully as she caught her breath. Sweat trickled down her chest as she stopped in below the trick of light. Ada clapped. She did not know she was crying.

"You do that," the dancer told Ada.

"How?"

"You ask yourself, and you come back."

Ada closed the door behind her and felt the warmth of afternoon. She would walk home slowly, take a nap, and then face the rest of the day. She was restless. After the dance she understood. Loneliness. She did not expect to feel it—not here, not now. She was never lonely, or never aware of it. Maybe she always was. Maybe that was the reason for her addiction to adrenaline—the new, the rush, the deadline, the goal. But she loved living that way. And she had wanted to come here alone, to forgo the social scene in favor of her own solitude, just for a month. Maybe it was too much. Maybe she was not as good company as she thought. Was that the reason for the speed at the expense of reflection? Even yoga and meditation were scheduled in, fresh-brewed kombucha with friends after classes and then gossiping at farmer's market, everyone cooking together afterward.

She missed it. She was surprised. She had craved solitude, and now the silence was killing her. Silence. Was there anything more painful? Cold. An *oubliette.* Darkness. And her voice? Did she have one if there was no one there to listen?

It was not only that. Her being alone seemed to make people uncomfortable. They stared; one in twenty was motivated enough to approach, say something in one language or another. Sometimes she pretended not to understand. Sometimes she played along for a block or two. Other times she was blunt. She mastered, "I do not want to talk to you," and more effectively, "Fuck you," in several languages. But, really, she hated being a bitch, so she went back to her old standby. She told them that she was a lesbian and that her girlfriend had just died. It was simple. She found their various reactions amusing.

Society did not want women to be alone. Ada rejected this view, though not following protocol was exhausting. It attracted too much attention. But she only had one life. She refused to live it for anyone else, especially societal consensus. It was the worst in restaurants. It was as if the act of eating alone was an offense to mankind, especially the man in mankind. Ada could always eat at Mario's restaurant, sure, but she needed to cut that off, really. He made her laugh and forget why she was there. They were comfortable together, and it was easy. She was not there for easy. She was there for herself. Nothing from home. If she kept things up with Mario, Paulo might as well come over. Then she could be taken care of and forget the madness of the past.

22

Before her parents divorced, Ada lived in an old bungalow in Santa Monica, California. Her memory was selective of those early, happy days. Christmas, birthday parties, stained glass, an old calico cat named Oscar—this was what Ada chose to remember. Her room faced the back garden. The window was large and overlooked the lawn and a huge old tree her mother strung with lanterns. In the center of the window hung a long, slender, stained-glass window. Although it was small and out of place, Ada would stare at it from under her sheets during her parents' loud parties. She always had to go to bed extra early on weekends. She could never fall asleep. She did not mind. The lights from the lanterns sparkled through the stained glass. She lay and listened. The guitar, the laughter, the clinking of glasses. No, she would not let sleep come. The stained glass was blue and green, like a forest but for the glowing white fairy in the center. The colorless figure hovered over the darkness, floating, flying, her wings fluttering so fast that they disappeared into the hidden landscape.

Ada's dad had made the stained glass. He was an artist. Ada had once taken one of his small bronze sculptures to school for show-and-tell in first grade. When Ms. Olivier called home to express her appreciation for allowing Ada to share his art with the class, her father hung up the phone without saying a word. He left the dinner table and did not speak to Ada for several weeks afterward.

Ada passed the old cathedral without intending to go inside. Still, the stained glass drew her in. She took her camera out of her Chanel backpack. The light, the color, the contrasting darkness of the church walls. She took several shots. She would erase them. She took another. Then another. More angles, different light. *Jesus loves me. This I know.* The only time she ever went to church outside of school Mass was with Sarah. *For the Bible tells me so.* They would sing and make crafts. Sarah always copied Ada's artwork, even when Ada tried to hide her drawings. *Little ones to Him belong.* Ada's mom always threw the crafts away when Ada got home. *They are weak, but He is strong.* Ada lowered her camera and shot her wedge espadrille sandals on the stone underfoot.

Yes, Jesus loves me. The song stung. It was sincere, raw. It was something Ada would laugh at now—too sappy, too out of touch with reality, too idealistic. And yet it slapped her across the face. She remembered that she had once wanted it, before Estel. That she had believed in lyrics, in love, in salvation, in a higher law. But it was not true. No matter how good you were, you were never good enough. Jesus had left her in a trash bin. At five, she had wanted to believe. And that was the cosmic joke in spite of her mother. Innocence. Ada once believed completely. Every bit. Real. It crumbled.

Ada walked down the nave. She would explore every angle, every possibility. Light. Darkness. Color. Transparency. Shards of glass. Blood. Why couldn't she distract herself here? She and Jordan used to go to the California missions for inspiration. This was beautiful. Cold. The art. The design. The forethought. The craftsmanship. Admire. Drink it in.

No. The color fell in on her. What was she doing in a church again? She was not an artist anymore. She did not belong here. She was not good enough. She was a slut. What? She did not even believe that. Whore. She sat down on a hard pew. Fornication. What the fuck? You are not enough. You are shit. You will never be good enough. Ada looked up. Domed ceilings. The clear, clean sounds of prepubescent boys' voices. The church once the tallest building in town. Nothing greater. Supremacy. Remember you are not good enough. You cannot win.

Separation. Colder. "Ada, you do not belong here. Where do I belong?" Water. Downward plunge. Into the cold depths. Naked. Tangled in algae. Downward pull. The fairy strangled by her own wings. Sinking. Beauty is not enough. Lost. Insufficient. Passionless. Lacking. Fucked. Fucked from behind. Fucked from the top. Fucked by the priest. Fucked by the crowd.

To hear herself, Ada sounded like a lunatic. The reality of the feelings shocked her. Terror. "Here is my heart on a platter. What will you do with it?" She felt the soft lambskin as she reached into her backpack for a cigarette. Fumbling. She lit it before she made it out of the large, wooden door. A nun in a gray habit stared, as she brushed past.

Sunshine.

Jesus.

She was going insane.

She walked fast until she was out of breath. Then she sat on a bench in the park and watched kids play. A little girl pumped her legs as she got up higher and higher on the swing. Her braids bounced on her shoulders. Ada smoked as she rubbed her fingers in the indentations of the bench. She took a few photos of the inscriptions, graffiti, deeply cut lines in the wood, professions of love, angry protests. She put her camera back in her purse and found a sharpie. She took off the cap, breathed in the fumes, and wrote, "fuck fear" on her forearm. She slid her sandals off and walked into the grass. Kids played ring-around-the rosy five feet away.

"Take your shoes off," Ada said. She bent down to slip off her sandals and run her toes through the grass.

"Okay," Nathan said. He untied his sneakers while staring at Ada's feet.

"I love to stand barefoot on the earth. To feel her, to breathe her."

He studied her, paused, and then asked, "What do you feel, Ada?"

"A lot of different things. Strength maybe. Safe."

"I am happy to hear that."

"Thank you for bringing me here. I needed this. You have been so good to me in helping me get better. I know I would be dead

133

without you, but I forgot how much I needed this, to feel the earth, to touch her."

"It's called earthing. Your body essentially sucks in the earth's electrons. It's like a superdose of antioxidants."

"When I was little I made a pact with the earth. We had a terrible earthquake one night. I was alone upstairs in my bed. I was dreaming when all of a sudden I felt this rough jolt. I woke up, but it didn't stop. It kept going, shaking me. My head started throbbing, and I threw up. I couldn't even cry for help. I was so nauseous I couldn't move. I remembered from school we were supposed to take cover in the doorframe. I couldn't get there. Things were crashing all around me, and it was so dark. It was loud too, strange noises that I did not know. I curled up into a little ball and shook. Later I heard neighbors' voices. Someone banged on the door. I couldn't move. Finally someone broke in and came up and got me."

"Where were your parents?"

"My mom had already left my dad. I don't know where she was. We never talked about it. She came and got me at the neighbors' later that night. She gave me a warm bath by candlelight and let me sleep in her bed. Mine was still wet."

"And what was this pact that you made with the earth?"

"That I would listen to her if she would take care of me. I was so scared of her. Maybe I still am. When I listen to her, sometimes earthquakes happen. Maybe I cause them too. But when I take my shoes off in the grass and just breathe and listen, I feel like even when it all comes shaking and crashing down, I will still be okay. It's like getting stretch marks because you have big boobs. Not fun, but definitely worth it." Ada looked up at Nathan and blushed. "You must think I am talking nonsense at this point."

"That's the furthest thing from my mind."

Ada left the park. It was always easier to face the journal at lunchtime: discover a new restaurant, choose a table with good people-watching, drink wine, and eat squid. Ada could read, reminisce, and then flirt with the server to save her from madness. She would never throw the journal in public. She would not scream or fall into an abyss. She would simply bury the past in public. This time she found an old tavern, took a window seat, and ordered artichoke soup and a *fino*.

You are the reason. You are everything. You are me. I can't be me without you. I want to see you, feel you, breathe. I want you in every cell, every drop of blood, every whisper, every scream. If you were mine, I would never feel alone again. You are better than any drug I have tried, any fuck on the planet. I want you like I want myself. It's like you are me from another time. Maybe we were together in another life. I want you to be in the next one.

Ada could laugh in the tavern. She could make fun of herself, order another sherry, and strike up a conversation with the table next to her. She wished Kate was there. Kate called her out on her shit. That was exactly why Kate was not there. Ada knew that her shit was real. She would never share her journal with anyone. Those were her real thoughts. And deep down, Ada thought that maybe she was psychotic.

"Don't make fun of me. You remind me that I have a heart, and I don't want one."

Kate and Ada drank champagne and ate oysters in the Ferry Building after Sunday morning yoga.

"You are all heart, Ada."

"Are you mocking me?"

"Never. You go deep and that's why you pretend. Not everyone goes deep. Most don't. Don't worry. Your secret is safe with me. Everyone else can go on loving you as a bitch."

"No one loves me. I just scare everyone. Maybe I am just meant to be single because I can't please anyone."

"What are you talking about? What happened to you this morning?"

"Nothing happened. I got a new contract, and I met someone at Crissy Field on my run. It was a good morning. Don't change the subject. I don't please anyone, and so I'll end up alone."

"What the fuck are you talking about? You just told me you met someone. You don't please anyone?"

"No, not really. Well, with my body, yes."

"You are not exactly boring conversation, blondie."

"Okay, so I'm smart, pretty, whatever. But no one ever loves me for just me, so I am best single."

"You are the last person who needs to be single. What is this melancholy bullshit? Men want you twenty-four seven."

"So what if men want me? It doesn't mean anything. They don't really want me. They want some image of me, some idea. Sure, I play the part when it's a good one. It's fun when I like it. But fuck it if I ever start to believe that it's real. It has always been pretend, and the ersatz role is what makes it fun. I can do pseudolove, the game. The stakes are not high and winning does not take that much skill."

"Play the cold-hearted bitch, Ada. No judgment. You are happiest that way. No argument. But, Ada, the rest is bullshit. I love you, and I had to spend that long weekend snowed in with you in Tahoe, remember?"

"Yes, that was the real deal."

"That's when you told me your deepest, darkest."

"I never told you anything."

23

Ada paid the driver and stepped out of the cab. She looked up and slung her black leather jacket over her shoulder. The building was eight stories, narrow, ornate—a series of bricks, odd windows with rectangular pediments, wrought-iron balconies, and hanging vines. It stood in complete contrast to the floor-to-ceiling windows and gleaming steel of the modern apartments that flanked it. Ada pushed the code 4286 into the new keypad. The large, black iron gate buzzed, and she pressed on the hot metal. She studied the colors of the mosaic floor tiles as she walked inside—browns, tans, burnt orange, a splash of turquoise. She pushed the button for the lift and stared up at the twisted, bold chandelier as she waited. Once inside the lift, she adjusted the strap on her python sandals, straightening out the low neckline of her comfortable black summer dress. She took a couple of deep breaths. Elevators tested her resolve.

"Let's take the stairs.

"Are you crazy? We already bought the ticket for the lift."

"I don't care. I think it'll be fun. Don't tell me you're lazy now that we're in France. I like watching the muscles in your legs when you use them."

"And I like watching your ass from behind, so I'll take the stairs only if you lead the way."

"Deal."

Ada and Chris skipped the line to the lift up the Eiffel Tower. They began to climb the stairs, Ada setting the pace. Quick, slow, fast, teasingly. She would race up at full runner's speed, and when they lost their breath and started panting, their faces flushed and bodies beaded with sweat, she would slow to a torturous pace. She liked to bait him by lifting her skirt up in the back. Chris would inevitably grab her ass, and then she would start running hard again, laughing whenever he caught her and put his arms around her waist.

"Almost there," Ada said. They circled the second level, took the requisite photos, and then settled into the corner overlooking the Seine below. The view was vast. Ada was excited about life, of all that was out there. She felt it was all at her fingertips, that all she had to do was reach.

"I don't even feel afraid to be up here right now," she said. Ada leaned over the railing and put her arms up in the air. Chris grabbed her hips and squeezed her up against himself.

"That's because it's me you're feeling. Don't ever underestimate these biceps."

"Oh, I like these biceps," Ada said. She turned around and put her arms around Chris's neck. "But it's the Eiffel Tower. It's so strong and solid and big."

"I love your dirty mouth, Ada." Chris kissed her. She kissed him back hard and then sucked on his bottom lip before she pulled away.

"I know you mean me."

"If you were as big and strong and hard as the Eiffel Tower I'd want you up inside of me every day for the rest of my life. You'd have to be the one I married for that."

"You're not getting married, Ada."

"What? Why the hell would you say that? Why wouldn't I? Everyone does."

"You don't need to. You not only have this amazing, addicting, life-altering ass, but you're smart, that's why. You know you're too smart. What do you need to get married for?"

"What about love?"

"What about it?"

"Are you Ada?"

A girl stood right in front of Ada as the doors opened. Behind the girl, a tall, white last century door was left open to reveal the seamless continuation of the mosaic tile flooring into the entryway of the apartment. The building had been painstakingly restored. Ada was impressed. Mario's flat enveloped the entire floor, and there his daughter stood eagerly awaiting Ada's arrival with her messy blonde braids, a chain of daisies around the neckline of her simple summer dress.

"I am Ada." Ada smiled down at her. She reached for one of the girl's braids and then dropped it suddenly. "And you must be Fia. The way your dad talks about you, I have been so looking forward to meeting you, love."

"He likes you too," Fia said. She took Ada's hand and walked her inside. "That's why he's making your favorite—*fideuà*."

The entryway was large, with corridors running to the right or left. Straight ahead was an enormous mirror framed in jagged metal. Ada stared at herself and Fia, the two holding hands as they walked forward toward their reflections. Fia looked too old to be Ada's daughter. This was okay. It wasn't a bad idea. She could play auntie. Fia already liked her. It would be easy. Fia looked from their reflection and smiled up at Ada.

"You're really pretty," Fia said.

"So are you, sweetheart," Ada said.

Fia led Ada to the right down the long cool corridor. The ceilings were high, the molding detailed and white, like the stark, bare walls. They turned again to arrive in a large living room. Long, low, leather sofas ran the length of each wall. Large glass doors opened up to a wrought-iron balcony that overlooked the street below. Fia dropped Ada's hand and ran over to pick up her pencil from the floor. She sat down on the floor tiles and continued the drawing she was working on atop the wooden coffee table. Ada walked over to the balcony and studied the riot of green spilling over. Vines, variegated leaves, twisted, turning, herbs, and nasturtium. Tomatoes? An edible garden in the living room was like Mario.

"And the princess has arrived," Mario said as he entered the room. Ada turned to watch him walk across the long sofas, barefoot in worn jeans and a linen shirt, drinks in hand. Ada smiled as he joined her by the railing. She kissed him on the cheeks and then took one of the glasses from his hand.

"Sidecars?" Ada asked. She looked down at the orange peel in her glass and shook her head. "You have a good memory."

"Too good," Mario said. They clinked glasses.

"To old friends," Ada said.

"To Barcelona."

Ada took a sip. Vodka.

Ada had not drunk vodka for years. It was her go-to for a long time. Too long. Her party drink through grad school and the years afterward, when she apprenticed under and then assisted Jordan Follows. Jordan was a world-renowned freelance photographer whose kinky retro motel room shots were a favorite among collectors in Europe and Asia and sold for as much as the average American home. In the States he was better known for his travelscapes, his play of light and color unique enough to allow him to choose only the jobs and locations that most interested him. Jordan had taught a fall seminar lecture at UCLA when Ada was getting her master of fine arts. He told stories about how living on a sailboat as a teen had taught him about light and shadows. He entertained his students with explanations on how backpacking through Asia was the best way to learn color and contrast. He lectured on how their understanding of the photographer's versus the public's eye would differentiate them as either commercial photographers or artists. He used shots he had taken over the last thirty years to highlight his talk.

Ada listened to every word. She was enthralled the moment she saw the first photo—the gray stonework of the stairs off the Pont de Sully in Paris—and heard his deep, raspy voice, the long pauses he indulged in between words. When she stared up at the second photograph, a riad, the intricate pattern of colorful tiles, the curvature of the inner courtyard's wrought-iron balcony, she realized who Jordan Follows was. This scene had been ingrained in her memory, deeply buried in a place she seldom visited. The photograph was exactly the same, the context different. This was a lecture focused on travel. But this scene was too familiar. It was real. It was from her travels. She had seen it too often before.

Nathan's bathroom. Fuck. There it was in her mind. Every tile, the big soaking tub. The first couple of weeks he ran her bath for her, the water warm but not hot. He poured in whole milk from a glass pitcher and honey from an earthen jar. He lay out a plush burnt orange towel made in Africa and a black silk, monogrammed robe. The bathroom was white tile, floor to ceiling. The only color was the riotous chartreuse vine in the corner and the photograph that hung above the oversize tub. Nathan owned a Jordan Follows photograph. Riad. Nathan taught Ada the word but never spoke about the photograph. Jordan Follows's photograph, the image before Ada's eyes again at UCLA. Riad, the Arabian term for garden. It was a palace with an interior courtyard. The wrought iron of the barred windows of the photograph matched the vines of Nathan's bathroom. Ada had lay there night after night, caressing her naked body in the bathtub, praying she would heal, staring up at the photograph and imagining it was a Moroccan woman's initials on the robe that she wore to the bedroom each night.

Ada lost track of Jordan's lecture, but she went up to him immediately afterward and asked if he would have a drink with her. Spain or not, there was something in his work she wanted and was willing to get by whatever means. He said yes.

"We'll leave the sidecar conversation till later," Mario said, nodding over to Fia, who continued to draw feverishly in the center of the living room.

"I don't know that I want to hold you to that," Ada said with a smirk. "Or that may depend on how many of these you plan on serving me. Are you going to give me the grand tour?"

"Why yes, darling," Mario said, motioning with his hand and then taking her by the waist. "Right this way."

"You know all I really want to see is the kitchen, so show me your playground."

Mario led Ada down a stark corridor with vaulted ceilings. They passed through a series of double doors. First was a large study with wall-to-wall colorful cookbooks and mismatched library chairs surrounding a large, white, square table. Ada kept walking when Mario paused. No books right now, please. Farther down through another set of tall double doors was Fia's bedroom. Ada turned her eyes to the tufted linen daybed with ruffled pink bedding, a far cry from the modern aesthetic of the Mario she had known back in California. She stared at the dozens of drawings all over the walls, each tacked up with large white pushpins. They were primarily of the ocean. Ada smiled. Then a drawing caught her eye. It was another seascape, yet devoid of surf and sand. There was a baby in a glass jar, floating or sinking in the waves, like a naked test tube baby Moses.

"And why didn't you ever have children?" Ada asked.

She and Jordan sat at an old wrought-iron table in the courtyard of his backyard. Dim lanterns were strung above through the trees. The garden smelled of lavender. It was dusk, and Jordan had just lit a fire. They drank Montrachet and ate foie gras. It was their third date.

"I don't believe in children."

"They do exist," Ada said.

"I never had a need for them."

"What about love?"

"I'd rather love the whole world than a miniversion of myself. What a terrifying thought."

"But what about those sensational genes? You are a true artist, Jordan. You can't let them go to waste."

"Are you asking me to procreate with you, Ada? I am flattered."

Ada laughed. "You are just a genius, that's all. The world needs more of that."

"Less."

"What?"

"I am a monster. I will confess now. If I go on drinking this wine and looking into those eyes of yours, I will be lost. This is your last chance to escape."

"I hope you're hungry," Mario said. He turned around to find Ada still in Fia's room, staring at the wall above the bed. He stepped back inside and looked over Ada's shoulder. "Her mom lost a baby."

"Oh, I am so sorry, Mario." Ada averted her eyes from the drawing and touched Mario's arm.

"Not your trouble." He shrugged. "It wasn't mine."

"Oh, wait. Now we are talking on a whole new level. No one messes with my favorite chef. Do you need me to pay that bitch a visit and take her down when I get back?" Ada put her finger to her lips as if it were a pistol.

Mario laughed. "As much as I would like to see your kung fu skills again, Ada, I really am over it. Fia is my gift. I am a lucky man. Now let's get you another drink."

Ada looked down to see that her vodka was gone.

24

Ada sat on the acrylic barstool as Mario made her another drink. She dangled her stiletto from her toe as she looked around the long, efficient, air-conditioned kitchen. This was not the restaurant. It was cold and streamlined. The endless, spotless gray countertops were bare save for the vodka, cognac, triple sec, lemon juice, and orange Mario had taken out to make Ada another sidecar. Ada watched Mario as he dropped the orange peel into a chilled glass and poured her drink so high he was forcing her to remember.

"You are such a tease," Ada said as she took the glass Mario offered. After taking a sip, she licked the long trickle of alcohol that ran down her arm.

"What are friends for?" He winked. Mario broke open the orange and handed a segment to Ada.

"You are really going to press this, aren't you?"

"Ah, but this night is for you, my dear. And I am making your favorite—*fideuà*."

"Your trickery knows no ends." Ada took another sip and then threw her head back to laugh. Son of a bitch, this was too good to be true. She was out of Barcelona and back on her game. "Okay. You win. I won't even call you a bastard for you setting that stalker pilot on me or bring up the fact that you still owe me $2,500 in poker debt, and I won't make any references to the night that you took my purse and left me stranded on Abbot Kinney without my phone or a penny on me."

"You are very kind," Mario said. "And the walk did you good."

"If it weren't for this *fideuà* bribe, I would watch your back, Mario."

"Why do you think these stainless steel cabinets so shiny? Eyes in the back of my head."

"Would you start cooking, already?"

144

Ada watched Mario for the next hour and a half. She sat in a daze, happy, his one-man show visual therapy. Mario opened the refrigerator. He took out small shrimp, fish bones, clams, and mussels to make the stock. Then he bent down to the low cabinet beneath Ada, his pants sliding down slightly as he lifted out the heavy soup pot. Mario poured in some extra virgin olive oil, licking a drop that slid down his finger before he went to work chopping the onions.

Mario had made *fideuà* once before for Ada and their friends back in his modern compound in Venice Beach. Those days were pre-Jordan, post-Nathan, mid-Ada. Mario was married to Amy, the daughter of one of Hollywood's top plastic surgeons. Amy modeled and painted. Mario was the chef of the hour. They were gorgeous. The whole party was, really. Ada was invited because she ate so much spaghetti and drank so much vodka at Mario's bar during graduate school that she became the face fixture of the restaurant. Ada ended many a night with the front of the house and became good friends with Mario as well. She did not even know what *fideuà* was when she got there. She only knew there would be beautiful people, top-shelf alcohol, and a party till dawn.

"What is it that we are making?"

Ada leaned over the counter of Mario's all-white kitchen, a fuchsia orchid on the island the only pop of color. The house was only blocks from the restaurant but a world away. It was minimalist, glass walls, floating steel stairs, terrarium courtyard, and lounge on the roof. Ada had just finished finals. Her favorite professor praised the project she shot at Big Sur, primarily the image of the dying butterfly atop a cold boulder. Now, as a DJ set up, the scent of saffron started to rival that of the pot. Someone slapped Ada's ass.

"It's fideuà, Ada, a cross between risotto and paella. Now leave the cooking to the men," Mario said. "Go get your bikini on. The girls are in the hot tub."

"Bossy. I just got here. Can't I get a drink first?"

"Get this woman some vodka. Jeff, make Ada a sidecar. And keep your eye on her. She's my best customer. She gets the royal treatment."

"I'm on it."

Jeff became Ada's personal bartender for the night. He was a pilot, build like a marine, terrible company, but skilled at slicing orange peels. By the time the fideuà was ready, Ada was topless on the roof. She did not remember the rest of the night, except for dancing on the dining room table, and Amy locking her in the gray-tiled bathroom.

"I thought you were engaged."

The broth had simmered for nearly an hour. Mario strained it through a mesh sieve into a well-loved pot. He took out the fideus and placed them in a roasting pan. He drenched the noodles in olive oil, running his fingers through them thoroughly. He then baked them until they were golden.

"I am engaged."

"Why aren't you wearing a ring?"

"Oh, I guess I left it on the nightstand."

"Not big enough a diamond for you?"

"Something like that."

"Another drink?"

"Please."

Mario was a fast bartender. He made another drink for both of them and then began to add the toasted fideus to a wide hot pot on the stove. He ladled the hot broth over the noodles and brought them to a boil. The kitchen smelled of saffron and sex in the pantry on the coast. The fideus simmered, Mario stirring them between drinks and looks at Ada, occasionally adding more broth. Finally the two just stared at each other.

"Don't think I won't pry," Mario said.

"What is it like to be married?"

"If I stop to answer that one, we won't be eating until tomorrow."

"I mean, is it just a trade-off? What happens with sex?"

"This is why I love you, Ada. You are never really asking any other question except what is life like without sex."

Mario dropped handfuls of mussels into the pot and used the wooden spoon to submerge them. He opened his refrigerated wine cellar and selected a bottle of Priorat Garnacha Blanca. As the mussels opened, Mario quickly sautéed large prawns and took out three large shallow bowls. Every time Ada tried to help, he swatted her hand away. He was beautiful to watch. Mario took out his corkscrew and opened the bottle of light gold wine. He poured a sip for Ada to taste. It was rich, textured—the alcohol high, but well balanced.

"Velvety, apricot, green apple," Ada said.

"You like?"

"Very much. Shall I find Fia?"

"Yes. She calls this my cauldron."

"A cauldron full of prawns? Good man."

Ada wandered down the hallway. She peeked her head into the living room. There was a warm breeze through the open outside doors. Fia's pencils were on the table. Ada walked over to look at her drawing. It was a seascape, mainly blue except for the red on the shark's mouth. A topless woman cried on the beach. Fia was on the balcony. She looked down on the street below. The juice of a tomato ran down her wrist.

"Are you ready to eat, sweetheart?" Ada asked.

"Do I have to?"

"I thought the cauldron was your favorite."

147

"I think it's for you. I want to draw. Will you ask Daddy?"

"Of course. I like a girl who is focused on her work."

"Don't tell him about the tomatoes."

"Promise."

Ada found Mario in the kitchen. He had poured the wine and was ladling the *fideuà*.

"You could have them back."

"Let her draw. I remember those days."

"We have two of those difficult creatures. I'm happy one is eating."

"Make that two. We have an artist in the house."

The dining room table was red, the dishes white, the room spacious—except for the cacti in large white pots. A myriad of lightbulbs hung down from the ceiling. They ate, reminisced, laughed, and teased each other. Mario tried to convince Ada to move in with them for a year and work from Barcelona. Ada told him she would if he cooked like this every night. Mario brought out more wine, and late in the night Fia came in and climbed up into Mario's lap. She laid her head against her dad's chest and stared at Ada.

"Ada, will you tuck me in?"

"Of course, love."

Fia reached over and took Ada's hand. Ada stood up and set her napkin down on the table. Fia climbed down and led Ada down the hallway and into her bedroom. The room was dim. There was a shell nightlight near the open window. Fia let go of Ada's hand to put her kitten pajamas on. Ada looked around the room and walked over to the bed. She pulled back layers of pink and ran her fingers along the lace of the pillowcase. Fia ran over and jumped on top. She pulled Ada down. Fia started to laugh, and she hugged Ada. Ada rolled over to her side to face Fia and studied the freckles of her nose.

"Do I read you a story?"

"You tell me a story."

"I tell you one? About what?"

"About what you want."

"Okay. Give me a minute."

"Or we can play the genie game."

"Let's go with that. I like games. Genie away."

"I get to ask you three questions, and you have to tell the truth."

"Or what?"

"You just have to."

"I don't remember this game, but I can learn. Number one."

"Do you like my dad?"

"I think you are the luckiest girl on the planet to have your dad. Two."

"Fia means fire. What does your name mean?"

"Noble."

"Why are you named that?"

"My mom wanted me to be the very best. Three."

"Are you going to live in Barcelona?"

"No. I go back to San Francisco next month."

"Why?"

"That's where I live."

"I want you to live here."

"The weather would be nice. How about you visit me sometime?"

"Okay. Sweet dreams, Ada."

"Sweet dreams, Fia."

25

Mario did not wake Ada. She and Fia lay face to face on the same pillow. Mario pulled the covers up over them and turned the nightlight off. Ada did not wake all night. She tried to but could not. Full consciousness would not come. The hours swirled by, a medley of nightmares, dreams, wishes—past, present, future, torment, hope. She was six, sixteen, sixty. She did not know. It did not matter. It gripped her, played with her. She was a child. She was old. She was all the Adas in between. Fia's steady, heavy breath was her bedrock, girlhood trust, magic.

"Don't you want to get locked up inside here with me?"

"Why are you hitting the emergency button?"

"I like elevators."

"Why the elevator?"

"Which do you like best?"

"The brunette."

"Because, Ada?"

"She looks exotic, Moroccan."

"She could easily be French."

"Shut up, Jordan, and buy me a lap dance."

"What does the song mean, Mommy?"

"It means that she was free. The fire in her heart kept her free."

"Free from what?"

"From anything but her own spirit."

"Can I swim now?"

"Yes. Forever, baby."

"You can't come over, Ada."

"Why? It's brunch and volleyball day."

"It's Easter."

"So. I can't come?"

"Not this year."

"Fuck it, Sarah. How many times can I apologize?"

"Are you lost?"

"No, I'm looking for someone."

"We didn't pass anyone for the last hour."

"That's okay. There's a boulder that we meet at."

"There is a big storm coming in, sweetheart. Don't wait too long."

"Nathan, do you think you'll always live in Barcelona?"

"Don't know."

"Where else would you go?"

"Not sure. Anywhere else and I'd still have to come back."

"You love it that much?"

"I don't know about love, but part of my soul is here."

"I don't know what that feels like."

"You will."

26

Ada stared into and sometimes through windows as she walked along the narrow streets to pick up Fia. Two mornings had passed since she saw Fia and Mario. She had promised to come back and take Fia on an outing. As she walked, she was not window-shopping, merely diverting her eyes from passersby. Nothing was of consequence. It all looked the same after awhile—small produce markets, shoe stores, beauty salons, antiques dealers. Then Ada rounded a corner and saw a small, pink bootie through the diagonal glass, a onesie, a cradle. Fuck. So precious, so small, so beautiful. A woman walked out of the shop with a stroller. She trapped Ada from speeding by. Her baby was blonde, chubby, chewing on her fist as she looked up at Ada.

"You are so beautiful, sweetheart," Ada said in Spanish. She flashed the baby a big smile and then made eye contact with her mother.

The woman smiled, obviously proud of her daughter, wrapped up in her little world of naps and play dates, and what else was it they all did? Ada really did not know. She only knew that everyone wanted it. Even Mario. Her friends had spent countless dollars to start their families and then countless more once they had begun. Ada looked back at the shop window and felt sick to her stomach. She was supposed to want it. She was culturally, socially, and biologically supposed to want it. Look at Fia. Don't. When she looked at those tiny socks, all she felt inside was fear. An old, nameless, raw, cold fear that separated her from the world of womanhood that bonded in the propagation of the human race.

"I don't want a little me," Ada told herself as she kept walking. "I don't even want a dog. Fuck me. Am I that heartless?"

She bought the best baby shower presents, was ever the favorite auntie of her friends' children. But the thought of someone else inside of her, depending on her, growing inside her womb, caused Ada to stop breathing. She stopped for a moment on the corner and leaned against the stone wall. She rubbed her temples and tried to be reasonable. Let it all go. Forget about it. No one was insisting she have children. She was safe now. But the last time. No. Walk, Ada.

Two hours later, Ada sat in the back of the cathedral. She did not want to get close. She wanted to go unnoticed, to disappear, to think. Fia wandered around freely, her eyes scanning the stained glass until she found the contrast in shapes she was looking for. Fia looked a natural, her sketchpad, the artist, nothing to weigh her down, innocent inspiration, no expectations, no baggage—just a pencil and a creative brain. Ada felt a hollow tinge of pain to remember those days. She looked up. How did the ceilings go up so high?

"God, Ada. Look at that sunset."

"Grandma said that I'm not allowed to say that."

Ada and her mom sat on their favorite blanket in the sand.

"Say what?"

Ada wound the dial on her Swatch and then picked up her stuffed shark and made it attack her mom's stomach.

"I am not allowed to say 'God.'"

"That is because Grandma thinks it's disrespectful, Ada."

"Is it?"

"Who is God?"

"The man with the beard that made everything."

"A man made you?"

"No. A woman did. But Grandma said God made everything, and so we have to do what he says. He seems mean to me. I don't like him."

"Did you say that to Grandma?"

"Yes. She washed my mouth out with soap. I threw up."

"Tell me about this woman that made you."

153

"Mom, you can't see her, but she is more beautiful than anything you can imagine. You have to close your eyes and feel her, and then you'll know. If she comes out of the ocean, don't look because you will die. She is gold and shiny, and your eyes will burn off, and then you will burst into flames because she is from another world that breathes fire. Her name is Estel."

Ada held the gaze of a saint on the relief above and looked away. San Francisco, San Diego, Santa Barbara, Santa Monica. Ada never had a chance. It was not in her to be a saint. How could it be? She never really loved anyone, really. Well, of course her mom, like everyone did, but enough to be a martyr? What was that? Sacrifice? Did it even make sense? Perhaps it was just something certain people were born with. The willingness to die for someone. Not Ada. She opened the journal.

I can never stop again because if I do, then I will remember. Hell. I will keep running forever. When I get home, I will dance and study and take photos like Nathan taught me because it is always there when I stop and think. Hot knives. Eternal damnation. Separation. Lakes of fire. The realization cold and sharp, piercing me open. But the warm flow of blood it robs me of is dead when it hits the air.

Give me a dick and let me run. The warm moisture that comes from my open legs and backward bend is infinitely superior. At least my body is alive until it's over. And there is always another fuck. Please. If I stop, I will be dead. Don't ever let me stop.

When had she written this? What the fuck kind of insanity was this? Wait, that was written here. Oh my God. In this very cathedral, after the accident. She had come to try to repent, to heal. She had come to ask forgiveness for what she had done, for what she was going to do. But then she could not believe. If she felt guilt from then on, it would be her own responsibility. And her unbelief was not because of her mother. Yes, her mother would have lectured her for even being there, inside a church—a cathedral no less. The robes, the altars, the flicker of the purchased flame, slave masters of women, intellectual suicide, backbones turned serpentine. Do not think; just believe. Faith. Simple faith. Ada had wished for it that day. To be simple, like Sarah. Forgiven. She banished the thought as far as the east was from the west. Ada waved for Fia to come.

A cross. A crucifix? Organs, offerings, confessions. Ada watched Fia walk toward her, her braids bouncing as she smiled. A woman stood up and scolded Fia as she passed. Ada did not understand the words, but she saw Fia pull her skirt down and her smile vanish. The full force of Ada's anger came to her consciousness. Why had she brought a little girl to a church? She would not be controlled, would not be punished. Ada carved her initials on the hard wood of the pew in front of her with her Swiss Army knife. She was thirteen again. Rebellious and without reason. As if her defiling of church property would free her body and soul.

"Let's go, Fia. I'll buy you a gelato."

"Please, Ada, can we stay just a little bit longer?"

"You like it here?"

"Look." Fia held out her sketchpad. It was a rendering of zombie nuns in the style of stained glass.

Ada smiled. "Finish that sketch, beautiful, and then we are out."

"I just need a little longer. You can read your orange book."

"Yes, I'll do that."

I found her lipstick in the nightstand. It was red. I put it on. It was very bold. She must have looked like Cleopatra. I know she had dark hair. Nathan doesn't like blondes. I think the silk robe I wear still smells like her. I spilled some of my ylang ylang oil on it, but there is something else, like rose water. Anyway, I liked how bold her lipstick was on me. It was so red. Nathan was out having dinner with a friend, so I went into his study. I found an old folk album from Tangier, and I put it on the old record player in the bathroom. I still can't look at myself naked in the mirror. I hate my scabs and scars. I hate them. I turned the music up louder and went back into the study where there were no mirrors, only succulents, cacti, and book upon book. I took the robe off and tried to do the dance how she would have. She was so beautiful. She was curvy but not fat. She could walk straight into the room and make everyone love her. She was a scholar too. She was basically like Wonder Woman. With the lipstick on, I wanted to be her, so I just pretended I was her, and I did not look at my scabs or scars. I just danced. And then the most embarrassing thing ever happened. Nathan walked in. I wanted to die. He asked what I was doing in his office, and then when he saw me, he started to laugh. I really do want to die. Why didn't they just kill me all the way? Why did I have to be saved?

27

When Ada woke up the next morning, she already felt the heat on her cheeks. The window clacked open and shut. The breeze was strong and warm. The day would be hot. Ada remembered she did not have dance class today, and relief flowed through her body. She relaxed her tense, sore muscles and stretched her hands back to grab the headboard. She took a deep breath and stared up at the ceiling. It was already warm enough to walk around naked. She should swim in the morning and then lunch at her favorite new bar for paella. She could sleep through the heat of the day later and then go out when the sun went down.

Ada rolled over to lift herself out of bed. She twisted her ankles, stretched her hands up high again, and then bent over to pick up the journal and put it back in the drawer. Something fell out onto the tile floor. It was a photo. It was not one that she had taken. It was of her. Jordan had taken it. She was wearing a gauzy floral slip and was leaning against the front door of his bungalow. She did not remember having any photos of their time together in Venice Beach. Those days were so far away. And now the house was tainted. She would never go back. She couldn't.

Ada turned on the television to watch the news as she stretched out in the living room. The paramedics were taking Winston out on a gurney. Ada started to cry. She had not cried for years. Why was she crying? She sat down on her cowhide chaise lounge and leaned her head back to stare up at the dark beams of the vaulted ceiling. She did not even know him, really. That was another life, four, five years ago. She could think of at least one party they had both been to at the same time. It was out at the ranch. Santa Barbara. Death by asphyxia. Suicide. Fuck. Why? She knew why. This scared her. Was she crying for him or for herself? She did not want to think about it. Vodka? No, she would never get any work done this afternoon. Run? Maybe. But fuck it, she did not want him to be dead. It meant something.

157

Especially to die alone. She was happy Jordan was already gone. He was the one she had worried about, those depressed bouts after their best shoots. Even later, when she had moved to San Francisco, Ada would be the one to go to Los Angeles or New York to nurse him back or check him into rehab. Fuck it. And to think Jordan was the one who died peacefully on his boat in Sardinia. When Ada first got the news, she had naturally suspected Jordan of suicide. Of course it was. But after the shock wore off, and friends that had been there had called to explain, she counted Jordan as one of the lucky ones. He had fallen asleep in his suit after a long, wine-filled dinner with friends and never woke up.

Ada pulled herself up off the chaise lounge and began to pace the small room, tears running down her cheeks. Asphyxia? "Winston, what were you thinking?" She did not want to go there. "Cut it off, Ada. It is not your life. You do not cry. It is not your affair. Lovers were lovers; that's all." She had had hers, Jordan his. They were all connected in some way or another, but she could not fall apart like this for someone she barely knew. It did not matter. Then why did she care? One night of partying in worn jeans and boots and flannels. Horses, sea air, vineyards, the fire pit until dawn, and pinot noir so sexy that for a while she even swore off Burgundy.

Ironically, Ada owned one of the first pieces Winston had designed. She looked down at the large onyx cabochon gold ring on her right hand. That did not bother her. It was her first real gift to herself. It had nothing to do with Winston or her sobbing. He happened to be the designer, but she had met him in one of those small world moments after the fact. She had bought the ring at her favorite boutique on Melrose Avenue with her first paycheck from Jordan. It was symbolic. It was her freedom, her destiny. It was her full, pure commitment. It was her own engagement and wedding ring wrapped up in one. She would survive and take care of herself.

Ada saw the image of the gurney being wheeled down the walkway on the television again and realized where it was. Fuck it, he got

Jordan's old Venice Beach bungalow? Ada had lived there with her mentor when she was first starting out. She noticed the mezuzah on the doorway and the screen slamming shut behind the paramedics. She turned the television off. Ada walked into her bedroom and took off her ring and sweater. She needed to get out of there. She took off her bra and her yoga pants and threw them atop the charcoal velvet quilt on the bed. She needed to run. Now. No time to hang anything up or stay in her apartment another minute. It was a cold and foggy morning, and Ada had already been to barre class, but she did not care. She could run down to Chrissy Field, and if she still was not better, she would continue across the Golden Gate Bridge. When Jordan had died, she had run all the way to Sausalito and taken the ferry back. That made sense. He was her mentor and her lover. This did not. Winston was cannabis and some very good wine, nothing more.

She ran hard. Her lungs burned. Her legs ached. She realized she had only had a green juice and raw almond butter after barre three hours ago, but she sprinted on. Her cheeks stung. The water was choppy. She could not see out very far. Alcatraz was hidden from view. Just as well. She shivered as she sweated, her black track jacket moist against her skin. Run Ada. You can, and you will. You can, and you will. Jordan. Winston. That is another life. They cannot touch you here. You were right to move here. You have it made. The money is easy. Life is good. Ada was glad she had grabbed a pair of sunglasses on the way out the door. She wore them in spite of the lack of sun to mask her tears. No one had to know. She would be fine by her afternoon meeting. Fuck you, Winston. Fuck you.

"Jordan talks about you all the time." Winston passed Ada a joint. It was nearly three in the morning at the Santa Barbara ranch. They were the last two awake by the bonfire.

"Funny, he never talks about you." Ada rolled onto her back. Her flannel shirt flapped open to reveal her stomach. Winston leaned over and traced her bellybutton with his pinky.

"We all aren't lucky enough to be as interesting as Ada."

"You are full of shit." She slapped his hand away and took another drag.

"Answer me this." Winston took the joint back and kissed Ada's stomach. "What is the significance of the Swatch?"

"What Swatch?"

"Jordan showed me your work. I wanted to buy the shot in the bathtub. He said you wouldn't sell."

"No."

"Was it yours?"

"The Swatch was the last thing my dad gave to me. He got it on one of his trips to Europe, probably at the airport. I never saw him again. I never even knew that he died. I found out a few years ago when I was going through old art magazines for a college paper."

"Touching." Winston climbed on top of Ada. She pushed him off. He grabbed her. She wrestled him down until she was straddling him.

"Now you tell me something, Winston." Ada grabbed his wrists and pinned him down. "How long have you been sleeping with Jordan?"

Ada could see the bridge now, the top anyway. The base was shrouded in fog. She could feel its strange energy as she got closer. She was glad it was so foggy. She wanted to both be fierce and hide at the same time. She wanted to push her body in her full strength while letting the power of nature take her over still. The fog did that to Ada. It squeezed her, choked her, frightened her. It felt good. The Golden Gate's red silhouette looked rusted today, moist, sweating like Ada. It was a solitary morning. So quiet that as Ada passed the warming hut she was surprised not to see any dogs waiting out front. She could stop for scalding hot black coffee on her way back. For now she had to keep running. It was all coming back—the rawness, her life before commercialism. Back when she still had a chance to believe. "Fuck you, Jordan, for taking me there."

Ada slipped the photo back into the journal. She fell back down onto her pillow. She pulled the white sheet up over her head and shook.

28

The model gripped his forearm with one hand, his thigh with another. His skin was very dark and flawless. His stance was controlled yet vulnerable. He was naked—a blank canvas. Ada was the artist here. He was her work. She studied his torso. His abs were tight, impeccable. Ada wanted a struggle, not apparent victory.

"He is too perfect," she said. "Where are his scars?"

"You have to find them," Jordan said.

They were in Jordan's studio, the converted detached garage of his Venice Beach bungalow. Ada had moved in with him the week she graduated from UCLA, two months after they had met. She would study and work under him for the next year. She was book smart and knew how to work society, but according to Jordan this was not enough. There was more to her. Ada laughed at him, but she moved in anyway when he asked. It was his photography. It was another language. It was like he knew he had a soul.

"Some would glorify his beauty," Jordan said.

"There is more than that," Ada said.

"Show me."

Ada walked around the model. Gorgeous. That is what she would think if she met him at the pool or in Hollywood. But here? No. She wanted more. She did not want gorgeous. Gorgeous was not good enough. What the fuck did gorgeous even mean? If perfection was real, then it was not enough. "Show me something. Who are you, really? A face, a body, that skin. But what else? Where do you hide? You are naked a foot away from me." Is there such a thing as that level of freedom? What do you fear? The model seemed not to mind her walking around, studying him so closely. She could feel his breath. Mint. She was still not inspired. His nude body, pristine. She was not looking for Eden. Could she sit here like this and let a stranger circle her? Jordan had. She was comfortable nude like the model, but she was not perfect. She knew her flaws and how to manage them. Surely the model was doing this as well. She would break him. Ada sat down on a swivel stool and stared at her camera for some time.

"Why do we wear clothes, Ada?" Jordan asked, finally breaking the silence.

"On a practical level, for warmth."

"Practical in Saint Petersburg in winter, yes. It's eighty-seven degrees Fahrenheit today. Are you cold?"

"No." Ada looked up at him. His dark green eyes narrowed. She knew he would not let her out of the conversation until he had made his point. She wondered why she feared what that might be.

"Then take your clothes off."

"No."

"Why?"

"I'm not the model today."

"That's beside the point. I did not ask you why models wear clothes. I asked you why human beings wear clothes. You told me the primary reason is for warmth. That sundress you are wearing is practically a slip. You're not wearing it for warmth."

"No."

"Why are you wearing it?"

"Because I live in a society that forces me to wear clothes."

"Forces you. Interesting. If you had your own society on a planet somewhere, would you wear clothes?"

"Maybe, or maybe not. I don't know. I do like clothes because, well, fashion, of course. Clothes are their own language. I can express myself through them. It's fun. Then again, if I didn't have to wear them, I am sure I could express myself in other ways."

"I know you can."

"I don't mean like that, Jordan. I mean in the way when you speak French you express yourself through the French lens whether you are French or not, whereas if you speak Catalan you express yourself in Catalan. All words and languages are not the same when we translate them. It's the same with clothes. I don't know why people think they are, as if snake and serpent and serp all had the same meaning. They don't, because when we say those words we are not just talking about the creature itself. The word carries all sorts of deeper meaning born out of the culture and our own experiences within that culture. Sounds communicate more than a simple definition of an object. The language always conveys a deeper meaning and understanding of that object based on societal and historical context. It's the same with nudity. I mean, do you think society could handle being naked all the time, or would we just be fucking every which way?"

"So you think we wear clothes to ward off sexual temptation?"

"I'm sure that's one reason society enforces it, especially this one, yes. They are scared."

"What is that fear, Ada?"

"Scared of everything. Scared of themselves, scared of their own bodies. And yes, scared of fucking, fucking for real."

"Scared of fucking?"

"I'm not sure. Rejection? Maybe they're ashamed of their bodies. No. I don't know. Maybe it's the opposite. Maybe they fear their own beauty, their own power of seduction. Happiness. I think we fear happiness. We're afraid it's not real, or it won't last, so we ensure that it doesn't."

"Is that your fear? Happiness?"

"Yes. No. I don't know. I think I'm happy. Why shouldn't I be?"

"You are, but you are also afraid."

"Of what? I do whatever I want. Why do you say that?"

"I didn't say you weren't brave. You have nightmares, Ada."

"Everyone has nightmares, Jordan, even you."

"You sweat through your nightgown every night, Ada."

"What the fuck does this have to do with me taking pictures right now?"

"It's your lens."

"Then I'd better start shooting, hadn't I?"

Ada bit her lip and stared down at her camera. She would not cry. She would not let his words enter any deeper than they already had. He did not know her. Not really. He thought he was some sort of sage, a diviner. Really he was just a celebrity photographer with talent who wanted to fuck her. She would learn from him and become great. Learn, Ada. Bite your lip, shoot, and learn. She would take her photos and block out the images each time they came. She would use the model, his beautiful body, his smooth, dark skin, his expressionless perfection. Maybe that was it. Expressionless. Perfection was expressionless. The throat. She focused on his throat.

"Why do you have so many shots of his throat?" Jordan later had asked her, the images scattered out over the long tree trunk that was the dining room table. She had shot these old-school, with film. Jordan had taught her how to develop them himself in his darkroom. She liked the process, the part she played with her eye and hands each step of creation.

"His throat?" Ada asked. "They are not all of his throat. Look at this one."

"It's from behind, yes, but his head is turned, and I can see the silhouette of his throat."

She had pictured him being choked, the expressionless beauty leaving his face. His eyes wide, his mouth gasping in vain for air that would not come, the color of his skin changing slowly. His lifeless body finally limp. No more veins bulging through his muscles, no more supple skin and curved buttocks. The Adam's apple off to one side, fingernail marks pink in his neck, brown and red swirled together as his dark flesh was torn.

"I have a game I want to play with you," Jordan said. "Tonight."

Ada threw the sheets off her naked body. She knew she should get up, eat something, but she didn't want to. Jordan would be ashamed to see what she had become. If he were to see her work, her magazine spreads, her portraits of women in white, what would he say? Would he say anything? Or would she just see sadness in his eyes? More likely he would be furious. He would see her talent and tell her she did not deserve it, not like this. But she was making people happy. Her work was peerless, and she captured some of the happiest moments of the human condition. And with the money she was making, she was happy too. Wasn't that the bottom line? To make a living? She was glad Jordan was dead.

Ada tied up her Nikes and ran down the stairs. She would sweat all afternoon, anyway. She would be better with a run. She sprinted toward the harbor. This would be a fast run, a burn everything out of her body so she did not go insane run. Her lungs burned. She wanted her legs to burn too. She wanted to remember why she was Ada and why she was alive, and why she was not Winston, and why she was not dead. Why was she even thinking about this? So what if she had seen the photo of the bungalow? She should be happy she did not inherit Jordan's home. And Winton's work was different. He lived his art, his soul, and was successful. But look where it got him? Winston was dead. Ada wanted to live. She could not, would not, shoot like she used to—not here, not in San Francisco, and definitely not in Barcelona. And that was why she stayed away from the past, except for this trip. It was her only safety.

"Why did you choke him? Why not crucify him? Or burn him? Why use your own hands? Why the throat, the breath?"

"They are just pictures, Jordan. You make me sound like a murderer."

"Are you?"

"No!"

"Then why is your model dead for the show?"

"I don't want to show these, and I don't know why he is dead. He was too perfect, and I needed him not to be."

"He wasn't perfect."

"Well then, maybe I just didn't like him and wanted him dead. This is crazy talk, Jordan. I'm not a psychologist. I was using the model to tell a story, and that is the story I told. If you ask me to psychoanalyze myself every time I shoot, then I am running away."

"From what?"

"You."

"You are not running away from me."

"Fine. I used my hands because the crucifix seems to have lost its meaning. Burning at the stake? I picture myself being burned at the stake. But it's all been done before, Jordan. Where is the shock?"

"Is that what it is about to you? The shock?"

"I just feel as though everything has already been said before."

"Maybe. But not by you."

"Why would anyone care what I have to say? People want pretend, not real."

"The pretend take care of the pretend. There's more to you than that. What is your altar, Ada? Where is your holy place? How do you worship? Explore that. Choke that."

She had run farther than she intended. She was lightheaded. She felt high. It did not matter. She should stop for coffee and walk the rest of the way back. She needed a distraction. Running was not working the way she wanted. It was not strong enough, even seven miles in. She wanted to burn out the pain physically and then go have lunch—or dinner, by that time—clear-headed and in control. Instead, memories that she had buried away with Jordan's death were coming to the surface in a way that made her hate Winston even more. Fuck Winston for taking that photo and for killing himself. She should be sad, but she was angry. She would not die like him. No. Safety first. Espresso. She would let the memries come until she made it back to the apartment, and then she would erase. No more. No more Winston. No more Jordan. Her career was most important. Her shoots made the international female populations of the modern world happy. What was wrong with that?

"Dom Perignon? What's the occasion? I thought you were mad at me."

"Mad?"

"For the photo shoot today. You weren't happy with my shots."

"On the contrary. Those are the first real shots you've taken."

"How can you say that? What about my graduation project? The portraits."

"Beautiful, yes. Passable for art, maybe. Real, no."

"That's not what you said at my show."

"At your show I specifically told you that your photography was as breathtaking as you are."

"So I am not real?"

"Not always, no."

"Fuck you, Jordan. You know Dom Perignon is my favorite, so you bring out a bottle to feel better about telling me I'm fake? Are you trying to make me feel like shit or just ruin my night and then get me drunk?"

"Tonight is about you, Ada."

"About me?"

"Yes."

"Enlighten me."

"What you shot today, Ada. It was only the first layer, but it was you. If I did not know you had so many layers waiting to peel back, you wouldn't be living here."

"Oh, thanks. So now I am some project of yours. Barbie on the outside, tragic American sweetheart on the inside."

"You are no sweetheart. And if you were, you wouldn't be living here."

Did she still have those shots? She knew she did. She knew exactly where they were too. They were with the others. The others she shot the night before she left Jordan and drove all night, driving, driving until she ended up in San Francisco and decided to find a place to start fresh and live free of the past. The photos were carefully packed in her Louis Vuitton trunk in her living room in San Francisco. They were safe inside archival envelopes. She had carefully stored each one. She refused to look at the images as she drank a bottle of sparkling wine from Carneros and listened to Sabicas late one night as she made plans with herself. She would not look at them. She buried them below the journal she would not read until she went to Spain the next summer. Yes, she would go to Spain. Ten years. It was her anniversary, and she would celebrate. She had just bought her ticket, first class, Virgin Atlantic, July seventh. But Jordan, no, he never saw them. No one had. And no one would. She would destroy them when she went back home. Then she could bury them along with Barcelona and move on for good. If Jordan had seen them, she knew what would have happened. That is why she had to leave him. He would have published them. He would have held a big show for her too, in spite of her protests, and she never would have been able to become all she was today. He would have completely exposed her. She was right to have left.

"When I say tonight is for you, Ada, I mean that completely. You have to trust me. Tonight is for you. I am a happy and willing witness, yes, but I am nothing more than your pawn. It is your show. You are on stage."

"Jordan, is this one of those acting exercises you like so much?"

"Ada, you are an artist."

"I am a photographer. I want to be a photojournalist, to travel, explore. I am not an actress. The photos I shoot are people, places. I know I have talent, but really, I don't think it's quite as deep as you make it out to be."

"There is more in you than commercialism."

"Yes, but I want to make a living too. I can take photos for my own pleasure, but I need to be able to take good ones to sell. You know that, Jordan. Magazines, clients, weddings."

"Fuck the thought of weddings, Ada."

"People pay a lot."

"And now you're a whore?"

"Fuck you. No."

"Then show me. What are you?"

Ada stripped down once she was back in her apartment. She threw her soaked clothes onto the bathroom floor and walked into the kitchen in search of food. She opened a drawer to take out a spoon and opened the refrigerator and took out a jar of almond butter she had made from the almonds she bought at La Boqueria. She scooped the spoon into the creamy, raw mixture, feeding herself bite after bite as she leaned against the kitchen counter and finally fell asleep on the rug.

"You are playing a game you may not survive," Ada said.

"That is exactly why I am playing it."

"Give me the key to the studio. And, Jordan, don't look for me unless I don't come back by tomorrow night."

29

The next day, Ada opened the taxi door and climbed out onto the sidewalk in front of the restaurant. She paid the driver and grabbed her bag from the back seat. She threw it over her shoulder and scanned the facade. She laughed. It was sexy. This was her first commercial shoot in Barcelona. First? Let's not get carried away. But she was working in Barcelona. She was in control. There would be no variables. This was easy. Mario met her at the front door. She kissed him, and he led her inside to a table in the courtyard. Ada sat with her back against the brick wall and looked out into the crowd. There was not a table free. Mario wore his chef's apron. A server brought over mussels and a bottle of Priorat *rosado*.

"Cheers, bella." Mario clinked his glass against Ada's. They took a sip of the Garnacha rosé. Ada smiled at Mario as she reached into her bag.

"Proud of you, Mario. This place is on fire."

"You know it's my passion. Hence Fia. I am just happy to do what I do."

Ada snapped a quick photo of him.

"Not of me, Ada. Focus on the restaurant."

"You are the restaurant. And everyone loves a toothsome chef. Trust me."

"That I do. I am at least that intelligent. I will let you do your thing and get myself back into the kitchen. *Mi casa es tu casa*. Let me know if you need anything at all. Your wish is my command."

"Be careful with that one."

Ada took another sip of the robust rosé and sampled the fresh mussels. The afternoon passed quickly. Ada did what she did best when she was working. She captured movement. She told the stories that people missed but wanted to read. Ada shied away from shots that were stagnant or clichéd. She found perfection in imperfection. Ada showcased Mario's cuisine, not by stylized plates of colorful minifeasts, but by evidencing people's interactions with the pleasure his simple creations gave them. Unblemished shots were not Ada's predilection. She found beauty in wrinkled hands slicing seared scallops, Carignan-stained teeth, and bartenders too busy invoking pure joy to check their posture. She almost felt happy as she sat down at the bar after several hours on her feet, asking for a glass of Priorat red blend.

"Ada?"

Ada stopped. Her heart fluttered. She looked at the bartender and could not move. She recognized that voice, like something from another life—something so deep inside of her that she could not erase its traces. She did not want to turn around. She took a breath. It was her imagination. She felt a hand on her back. No.

"Ada, is that you?"

She turned. "Nathan?"

"Jesus, Ada. You grew up." He kissed her cheek and then bent over and hugged her. Her body melted into his too easily. She was plummeting. This could not be happening. It could not happen. This part of her life was pretend. It did not happen. She did not want proof. She had to erase this. She stood up.

"Wow. How are you, Nathan?"

"My god, Ada. You look fantastic. You are what I want to hear about. I am just plain old, same me."

Ada wished she could say that. Just plain old Ada. Who would that be? She stared at Nathan's jawline as he talked, imagined her mouth on his neck, her tongue tracing his sideburn as she slid herself down onto him. Fuck. Maybe she was just Ada.

"Mr. Interesting? I am sure you could out-story me in a flash."

173

"I would take you up on that challenge now if I could. I am heading out to a meeting and then have dinner with a buddy tonight. Do you still like guitar? There's an open-air flamenco concert tomorrow night that I was thinking of going to. Come?"

"I love guitar." She hated guitar. She wanted to bash a guitar over his head and send him back into her imagination. She wanted to take cold, taut guitar strings and strangle everyone on the Iberian Peninsula until it was a wasteland that no longer existed. No, she loved guitar. She wanted to straddle him as he played, his fingerpicking sliding off onto her inner thighs. Fuck. She was saying yes. She would go.

"What time?"

"Nine. Shall I pick you up? Where are you staying?"

"I'll meet you there."

"Sure. Do you remember that bar in El Born we used to go to on weekends?"

"To get your vermouth?"

"Exactly. That's the one. It's right around the block. See you there?"

"Perfect. No vermouth for me still?"

Nathan laughed. "Not for me, either. Looking forward to it."

He kissed Ada on the cheek, and she sat back down on the barstool. She looked at her glass. The wine was inky purple with an undertone of terracotta. She swirled it around and watched the tears run down the glass.

"Special delivery."

Ada slid her hand down from her hairline. Her head throbbed. The large glass doors were wide open. A warm breeze blew in from the balcony. She lay on an old cozy wicker daybed, the linen pillows tossed onto the terracotta tiles below. How long had she been lying there, her blank stare focused on the wrought iron and chartreuse leaves? Too long. Nathan was looking down at her now. He struggled to hide his furled brow with a smile. Ada shifted her legs over, and he sat down on the daybed. He held out a white paper envelope. Ada reached out her hand.

"Open it."

"What is it?"

"Open it."

Ada slid her finger underneath the flap and pulled out a stack of photos. There were twenty or so, matte, three by five. She propped herself up. Nathan leaned back next to her against the bed frame and watched her flip through the images. He had developed her photos. These were the first she had taken with his camera. Nathan's worn messenger bag on the Eames lounge chair in the living room. Her freshly polished toes in the sand on the beach of the Barceloneta. The neighbors' cat on the white bedsheets when she had wandered in.

"You should study photography when you get back to California."

"These are just random shots, Nathan. No one would want to see them but me."

"No, seriously, Ada. You have a great eye. Promise me you'll invite me to your first show."

"Sure. As if my mom weren't already going to kill me."

"I'm sure your mom wants you to be happy. And if you are this good at taking random photos, think of how that would feel to study and to do it for a lifetime."

"Let's go somewhere tonight. I don't want to lie here anymore."

"Give me one of your photos, and I'll take you to my favorite bar in El Born."

"Deal."

Ada climbed down onto the floor and knelt down to face the daybed. She spread the photos out into a collage of the last few weeks. She would not remember most of those days, just glimpses of memories. The tattered Berber rug. The morning sunlight on the cognac velvet sofa. Jars of honey on the sideboard. The moon from the roof at three in the morning. Cigarettes in the park. Garnacha by the fire. Nathan chose the shot of graffiti. The large cursive letters read "untamed." He said that was how he would remember her.

30

"Tell me about the worst girlfriend you ever had."

Ada sat and talked to the bartender. It was late. This was her third bar. She did not want to go back to her apartment yet. She speared a garlicky shrimp and slid it into her mouth. The bartender poured her a young white from the Penedés. It was bright and acidic. One more glass. The bartender was helping her forget. He was double her age and his stories were even wilder than hers.

"Nineteen seventy-two. Before you were born, I know. Blonde. A knockout like yourself. But bat-shit crazy. She once set fire to the kitchen when I asked to stay home one weekend. Wasn't good at confrontation. Avoided it by whatever means. Slashed the car tires because she did not want to come home from Sitges, threw my shoes into the ocean because I swam out too far, gave my cat to the neighbor when I had dinner with my mother. Terrible girlfriend. Nice legs. Now you top my story, and your drinks are on me."

"No house fires here. Mine was a lot younger than I was. Good in bed, but a raving lunatic when it came to sex. He had this thing where he wanted me to be a whore. He wanted me to go out on the town all night and pick up guys. The more the better. He would wait back in his apartment. I would come back, and he'd want me to tell him who I had met and what I had done with them."

"You beat me, blondie."

"I didn't do it. I thought about it. It's kind of a great setup, right? Sleep with whoever you want and then have a warm bed to come back to."

"You are no whore, blondie."

"If I sleep with someone it's because I want to, not because someone is keeping tabs. And I don't like to kiss and tell. My sex is for me."

"Brava."

Ada asked to pay her tab. The bartender shooed her away and turned his back to her. Ada left a tip on the counter and slid off her barstool. The group next to her was getting rowdy. She could have a nightcap at home. It was a short walk. The breeze was warm on her face. Ada dropped the key on the entryway console and walked to the kitchen. She grabbed the bottle of rosé, a glass, and made her way to the bedroom. She turned on the lamp and stripped down before getting in bed. She poured herself a generous glass of wine and tossed the journal onto the sheets. She took a sip before falling back onto the mattress.

I still run every morning on the beach. It's not the same. It has been three months. No more jet lag, no more blood, no more anything but college, really. I decided to live at home and drive in, no dorm, but still lots of parties. I like it better on the beach. The older guys are better. When I got home in September, Mom freaked out a little with me being back, but not too much. As long as I'm in school, she doesn't really care. Her girlfriend Carrie just moved in, but they're going to Italy during the remodel so I will pretty much have everything to myself. Carrie is a yoga instructor, so Mom has been making me go to her classes. It's fine. I can do the splits, stand on my head, and I'm working on my breathing. It's the running that is making me angry. I'm just as fast, but it's not the same.

Fuck. I'll just be honest because no one will read this, not even me. I feel it. I don't know if it's really possible, but I do. It's inside. It's not me, and I don't want it. I don't want any of it. When I run and it burns and I feel alive and my legs stretch and my stomach flexes and I know I have power and I can run forever … it hasn't been like that. It's eating me. If I don't do something, it will kill me. Is that bad? Kill or be killed? I don't think I want to die anymore. I want to live.

She took it in. Breathe. She took a sip of wine and looked down at her stomach. She touched her skin. No stretch marks. She traced her belly button and then propped herself up onto her elbows. She took another sip of wine and flipped over to read the passage again. She carefully closed the journal, set it on the bedside, and turned off the lamp. She stared up at the ceiling in the dark room.

Ada went back to Boston to spend Thanksgiving with Chris. It wasn't their plan, but he sent her a ticket, and she flew out. Ada really did not want him to see her, but she also did not want to spend Thanksgiving alone. Chris picked her up at the airport, and they ate at a pub on the way back to the hotel room he had booked. He had to live on campus, and Ada was already bored with the college scene. She had forgotten how good their chemistry was. It was easy to be with Chris. When he fucked her she was 100 percent her hungry self. No rushing, no pretending, no insincere words, just good honest fucking. In the car, in the shower, on the floor. Ada remembered what it was like to be herself again. Her breasts spilled out of Chris's hands, and she rode him hard. Damn, she had forgotten how good this felt.

"I think that's our record," Chris said. Ada lay naked on top of him with her head on his chest. "Five times in one day."

"Maybe six," Ada said. "Be prepared for me to wake you up in a few hours."

"What did you do to your body?" Chris asked. He grabbed her ass with one hand and her breast with another. She pressed herself down harder on him. She didn't want to move.

"Aren't I the same?" Ada asked. She held her breath. This is why she did not want to see him. This was the part she was dreading.

"There's more of you," Chris said, squeezing her again, "and I like it."

Ada slid off of him. She rolled over and faced the window. Chris wrapped himself around her again, but she would not look at him. She would not move. She just stared.

"Chris," Ada finally said. She knew he would be asleep in a moment.

"Yeah."

"I'm pregnant."

Ada did not wait for Chris to fill the silence. She did not want a reaction. She did not want words. She only wanted it over. She felt his hand settle on her waist.

"I don't want to talk about it so please just don't say anything. All I ask is that on my last day here you take me somewhere, and we erase."

31

Ada thought she was ready for flamenco this time. She actually wanted to go. She needed it. She could do this. She went in strong. No more bullshit. No more fear. Fuck fear. She would get a tattoo right on her hand, damn it. She changed quickly. She heard the strum of the guitar in the studio. When she walked in, she was surprised to see a man sitting there. It was not a recording. It was live. The dancer ignored Ada's stare. She corrected Ada's posture and led her through warm-ups.

"You ready."

"Yes."

"Now you dance."

"Dance? Now? Me?"

"Who else?"

"But what's the choreography?"

"You no need no choreography. You dance."

"What?"

The guitarist strummed. The chords were sudden, loud, forceful. Ada prayed. To whom, she did not know. Crucifix. She raised her chest and stretched out her arms. The guitarist stopped his playing and began to sing. The words bled, but they flowed easily. Embody me, Ada whispered. Hear me. I want your spirit. Give me your body. Your movement. I give you mine. Take me. Fill me. Flow through me. Resurrect, Ada. Raise yourself from the dead. No one else can.

Ada lifted her arms as the guitarist strummed again, this time harder. His voice was raw. Ada let him swallow her up. She let herself slide down into the sadness, the pain, the rage. She did not fight it. She let it flood over her and take her into its dark grip. Her body was swift, her movements violent but precise. She let her body seduce the space. Her gaze was far away, yet her body remained present. Her feet sped; she arched backward, clutched her chest. She spun across the floor, panting, angry, her tears hot. She spread her arms wide again, sweeping down to the floor before raising her chest up to the rafters and screaming. She panted, turned, walked slowly across the room, her eyes focused on her own as if she were her own prey. She stopped suddenly, fell back into a deep backbend and completely surrendered.

"Now you dance."

The dancer got up from her seat and followed the guitarist out the door, closing it to let Ada sob on the dark floor alone.

32

The night was warm. Ada wore a delicate, silk crepe tank dress and had left her jacket at home. The sea air smelled of jasmine. It felt like those hot summer nights of ripe, juicy cherries straight from the tree; dry, chilled sauvignon blanc from the outdoor refrigerator; and naked swims under the stars in her mother's black-bottom pool. They sat outside on the stone patio in metal cafe chairs. Some couples sat on the gravel pathways or on the grass surrounding the guitarist, leaning on each other or up against the stone pillars. The guitarist sat alone in the center, dark curls covering his brown eyes, his guitar visible in the candlelight against his clean black suit. Bottles of wine were everywhere—on the round tables, on the ground. People shared.

Nathan crossed his leg over his knee and stared at the guitarist's fingers. He wore a lightweight denim shirt and white leather sneakers. Ada breathed in his cologne and studied his profile out of the corner of her eye. He finally glanced over at her and smiled. He picked up the bottle of albariño at his feet to refill Ada's empty glass. The wine was chilled and tasted like wet summer sex on cement by the pool. The night was perfect except for the music. It was too faultless. Ada tried to breathe, staring at Nathan in spite of her resolve. His eyes were far away, locked on the guitar and yet somewhere else entirely. Alone. The feeling washed over Ada as she scanned the crowd again. The man to her left was sweating. He smiled at Ada, and she looked away.

Nathan was not there with her. She wanted him to stare at her that way, with whatever it was that sparked those glassy-eyed memories. The guitarist was lucky. He was aware of his guitar alone, his hands controlled and forceful, his body erect and expressive. A gold chain and cross yoked his neck; the hair on his chest was dark and clearly visible through his unbuttoned shirt. When Ada turned back to Nathan, she caught him staring at her. She blushed. Then her cheeks burned hotter to realize that she had blushed. What? Was she eighteen again? No. She was not. She did not look away.

"You like it?" Nathan asked. He put his hand on Ada's knee. She felt every inch of her throb.

"Very much," Ada said.

Nathan smiled and turned his eyes back toward the guitarist.

"What did she look like?"

"What?"

"Will you tell me what she looked like?"

"Who?"

"You know who."

"Ada," Nathan said. She watched his lips. So smooth, so soft. She wanted them on her. The words smeared on her body. He smiled at her. "I have no idea what you are talking about."

"Sorry," Ada said. "I think you can still read my mind."

"Pity I lost that."

"The woman with the robe."

"The robe?"

"The black silk robe. The one I used to wear."

He laughed. "I forgot about that robe. I think you wore it a month straight. I was happy when it ripped because I finally convinced you to leave the apartment to get some new clothes."

"It had a C on it. What was her name?"

"Catherine. She would have liked you."

"What? Really?"

"You are a lot like her."

Ada told Nathan she had to leave once the concert was over. She could not go get a drink with him. Not like this. He invited her to dinner on Friday. That would give her time to compose herself. Was it simply enough to have known love existed? Just this once to have tasted it on the very tip of the tongue? The raw aching. The longing. The satisfaction of some kind of strange completeness, even though she was alone in her love.

Companionship was not love. This is what she had believed love to be until now—the ability to be with someone day after day. The capacity to plan with somebody—meals, vacations, cars, houses, pets. Paulo. She had mastered this. Through Paulo she proved to herself that she could do it. She could be normal, like her friends—stable, able to cope with a shared routine. It was some kind of security that was agreed upon, polite society or not. But it was not love. Not like this.

This was a throbbing between her thighs accompanied by thoughts she had never known before. She wanted him to be happy, truly happy, whatever that meant. With her, without her, she wanted him to be the absolute fullness of who he was and who he could be. She wanted every part of him to be authentic and for him not to change for anyone, even for her. And yet she craved him. She wanted him in her bed, in her head, in her mornings and nights. But it had to be what he wanted. She would not try to make anything happen. It had to come from him.

Instead of reading the journal that night, Ada lit a cigarette and took out her pen. She lay down naked on her stomach on the freshly laundered sheets. She was afraid to write, afraid to record her thoughts. She got up and walked out into the living room. She finished her cigarette by the window, looking down at Las Ramblas, and then went into the kitchen. She took a bottle of rosé, a corkscrew, and a glass back to the bedroom. She lit a candle by the bed. She drank a glass, watching the flame. She poured herself another and then picked her pen back up. She stared down at the blank page.

I cannot handle that kind of ecstasy. He makes me so happy that he makes me so sad. It's like being cut open slowly, and all the blood draining out. I never knew such deep agony until I touched him. I forgot misery. And now there he is to remind me of everything I am not, everything that I do not have. I touch him or even just whisper his name and see his naked body above mine. And then I plunge. I become a stupid girl. I have a heart all of a sudden. A heart that would give up everything for this man who does not even know when my birthday is. But one night in his bed, and I am undone. I taste what I want my life to taste like, and I am willing to throw everything I have worked for away to be in his room, to feel his body warm next to mine as I give up sleeping alone.

Can that kind of happiness even be real? Maybe for a moment, a night? No. It cannot be true. It is pretend. They are only glimpses, small glimpses, of a fairy tale that can never come true no matter how sweet the voice and how patient the heart. They are the cruel taunting of the gods. They are my drugs. Indulge me one more time. I want to believe that the happiness can last, that love can last more than a night, but no more pain. The pain of you ripped out of me is fucking unreal. I don't want to feel. No, happiness is not worth it. Because I always end up loosing the blade and getting it stuck back in my heart.

33

The stage was dark. She walked in the darkness, an echo sounding through the empty theater as her heels hit the wooden floor planks. She could not see, but she walked forward, chin up, shoulders back, breasts lifted. The spotlight turned on. She was naked center stage, four-inch stilettos on her feet, a velvet choker with a rosebud tight around her neck. She looked out and breathed. She felt eyes. She saw no one. She let her head fall back, her arms outstretched. There was no music. She waited. Silence. She breathed in again. She lifted her hands to the rafters, arching her back until she came to the floor. She stretched her belly upward, exposing every part of her skin but the soles of her feet and the palms of her hands. Her stomach burned, and she held herself outstretched as she felt the eyes on her naked body. She took in a final deep breath until she collapsed onto the floor. She drew her knees into her chest and sobbed in the spotlight.

Ada woke up sweating. She sat up and lit a cigarette. The room was dark. She heard a car door slam down below. Ada ignored the dream. She played back the night with Nathan in her head. Catherine. She expected her name to be more exotic—something bewitching or defiant even. Catherine was elegant. Maybe that was why Ada seemed like a child to Nathan that summer. Catherine—long wavy hair, big brown eyes.

Ada blinked. She snuffed her cigarette out and got out of bed. She walked into the living room and stood in front of the open window. She could smell her perfume. It was on her body from the night before. It was one she had worn for years; the one that had taken her time to find; the one that had haunted her until at twenty-three she walked into a Paris boutique where she worked with an expert to create her own. Jasmine, ylang ylang, Moroccan neroli. It had taken hours, but the formula was right. Ada had it sent to her when she skipped her yearly jaunt to France. Orange blossom, tangerine, leather. But Ada's signature scent was a scam. It was a case of stolen identity. It was Catherine's.

Ada walked back to the bedroom and lit a candle. She breathed in the frankincense and then smoked near the open window. The breeze made her shiver. Catherine was never Moroccan. It could not be true. Ada was furious. She walked back over to the bed and stretched out. She stared up at the dark beams of the ceiling. She watched the smoke rise. She wanted the feminine dragon back. She wanted Python, the guardian of subterranean waters. She did not want Catherine. She wanted an accent. She wanted eyeliner and incense. She did not want a name that meant pure.

"Play the word game with me."

"Teach me."

Ada sat next to Wren in a dark corner of the Bar Marmont. She dangled her strappy, gold stiletto from her freshly polished toes. The glow of the bar was warm, the buzz intoxicating. But Ada could not have been happier. Her show had been, well, amazing. The gallery was packed. Most people had come because of Jordan, of course. Still, Ada felt the rush. Her cheeks were flushed as she and Wren clinked their Bellinis together.

Ada did not know she would sell her work. Of course she wanted the money. She just never dared think that people would actually pay for her images—images she had seen in her mind and then translated into poison that people wanted to imbibe. In reality, Ada wanted to keep her photographs, to guard them in her closet where no one could see them except herself. It was Jordan. He had tried to convince her to share, and when she refused, he put the show on without telling her. She was still pretending to be angry, so he had gone back home. Ada was not ready for sleep. Wren had bought the most gruesome of Ada's images and invited her back to her hotel for a drink.

"I show you my cards and you tell me the first word that comes into your head."

"Fun."

Wren reached into her clutch. She wore a low-cut silk jumpsuit. Her hair was short. The large gold serpent cuff on her wrist seemed familiar, but Ada could not place it. Ada took another sip on her Bellini and watched. Wren set a small black leather envelope on the dark table. She opened it and slipped out a thin stack of cards. Wren fanned the top five cards out face down in front of Ada. She put the others back in her envelope and motioned to the server for two more drinks.

"You can choose whichever card to turn over first. You are only allowed to say one word. Don't think. Don't analyze. Don't even try. Just speak."

Ada stared down at the five cards. The backsides were damask, a deep shade of burgundy. Ada took a deep breath and uncrossed her legs. Her white silk crepe mini dress tickled her legs. The fresh air cooled her sweaty inner thighs. She placed both hands on the table and looked up into Wren's eyes. They were green. Ada's heart began to pound, and she blinked. She looked back down at the cards. The server set two Bellinis on the table. Ada took the last sip of her first and handed him the glass. She then turned her focus back to the table and chose the card in the center. She stared at the gunmetal polish of her thumbnail and flipped the card over.

"Rape."

The image was of yellow ruler in a schoolroom. Ada forgot about Wren. She turned the cards over quickly in a horizontal row, left to right, one word per card. She spoke without hearing herself, consumed by the images.

"Cruelty. Pythons. Conspiracy. Sex."

Blood drops on a thermometer. Lichen on a boulder. A mattress on asphalt. Wren's cuff.

"Nice." Wren clinked her glass against Ada's. They smiled at each other and drank. "What does conspiracy mean to you?"

"To plot something out with someone, something secret, something that will probably hurt someone."

"Do you know where the word comes from?"

"The etymology? No."

"It's Latin. Con, with. And spirare, breathe. It means to breathe together."

"That's sexy."

"I have a bottle of Cristal upstairs."

Ada pulled herself up off the bed. She stretched her arms up to the sky and arched her back. She sighed and walked out into the dark living room. She fumbled through the playlist on the stereo. It had to be there. She could find something similar. The apartment vibrated. Ada lay down on the smooth floorboards. Her back and legs were cold against the wood. The breeze sent her empty cigarette carton to the floor. She shivered, her nipples hard. She did not move. She did not reach for a blanket. She felt cold down to her bones. She needed to remember that she was still Ada, that she was still alive.

"The game just changed."

"That's two words."

"Blind devotion."

Now Wren said the words that first came to mind. There were no photos—only Ada's drawings on the hotel room paper. They lay on the soft white sheets of the queen bed. Ada tore off the top page, crumpled it, and threw it to the floor. She propped herself up and looked over at Wren before she started to draw again. Her mind raced. Her body ached. Ada wanted her and wanted to be her at the same time. She was in bed with Barbie, only this Barbie was not merely ingenious. She was brilliant.

"Skinny snake bowels."

Ada laughed. Wren took the pen and flipped over to straddle Ada. She ran her finger down Ada's navel and then drew a butterfly around her bellybutton. It was nothing like Ada's game night illustrations. It was Keith Herring meets Tracy Emin. The butterfly was blissful, horny, and completely pissed off. Ada reached up and ran her finger along the cuff on Wren's bicep. It was coiled, the scales barely perceptible but like braille to touch.

"It was a gift."

Ada pictured his abs, the veins that ran down into his pants, his golden hair pulled back into a loose ponytail, his chin scruffy because he and Wren had spent the weekend in bed together on the coast. Wren took Ada's wrists and pushed them back onto the pillows. Her hands were cold, strong but soft. Ada arched her back. Wren folded and kissed along Ada's waist, skipping over the butterfly only to come back to lick its outline. Ada shivered. Wren kissed her way upward, lingering on Ada's large breasts. Finally they were face to face.

"To myself, Ada. The cuff never comes off."

"Gorgeous. It must have been made for you."

"The gods knew. Africa ripped my heart straight out of my chest. I held it in my hands until I got back to the States and found my freedom. On the flight home I was a mess. I drank whisky until they cut me off. I sat by a designer, Winston, from here of all places. He started ordering whiskey and pouring it in my Diet Coke. He told me to shed my skin, to be the serpent. He invited me to his shop, and when I slipped this cuff on, I forgot about Africa."

They never said another word until morning. They screamed, bit, wrestled, cried, but did not speak. Words did not matter. Lotuses should be eaten, not defined or explained. Neither slept until the sun had risen. Exhausted, sweaty, satisfied. Some time past noon Wren slid off the bed. Ada watched her walk to the window and open the shades. Her tan lines spoke of a recent trip to the beach.

"Can your Jordan spare you one more night? I say Veuve Cliquot, breakfast burritos in bed, and then a nap by the pool."

"Jordan can spare me for the week."

"I'm leaving tomorrow. I have to go back to Chicago to see my family for the holiday."

"The holiday?"

"Thursday is Thanksgiving."

"Oh, shit."

34

Each Thanksgiving, Ada's mom disappeared deep into the woods at dawn. Ada woke up in an empty bedroom, her granola poured out in a bowl on the wooden table in the kitchen, a sketchpad or new coloring book next to the jug of milk. Her mom did not return until dusk. Ada waited for her on the front porch in the woven rope swing, snacking on berries or walnuts. Her mom smelled of the forest, her clothes stained, her face smudged with dirt. She kicked off her hiking boots and then took Ada's hand. They walked through the door, and Ada's dad handed her mom a glass of champagne. He gave Ada sparkling cider. Her mom walked Ada through the bedroom and then stripped down in front of the large windows. She left her clothes in an earth-scented pile on the wood floorboards. She picked up her glass of champagne and sipped it slowly while staring down at Ada.

Ada did not drink her apple cider. Ada left it by the window as her mom held out her hand again for Ada to take. She led Ada into the large glass bathroom, and Ada lay on the heated floor tiles. She watched her mom brush her dark hair out of her face while staring in the mirror. Her mom's body was thin, her skin fair, her eyes always focused yet far away. She was beautiful. Ada stared at her and traced the lines of her stomach, her back, her breasts. Ada loved her, but she was continually terrified. Her mom did not say anything when Ada sipped from her glass of champagne. She simply stepped into the shower and started to sing. Ada looked from her mom's naked figure to the bubbles in the crystal flute to the myriad tiny tiles of the floor. Ada listened to her mom's haunting voice—the melodies familiar, the words sad, though Ada did not understand them. Later Ada's dad served dinner outdoors. They all sat around the fire pit and ate silently. Ada's mom drank wine from France and poured some into Ada's glass. Her dad drank something else, but he never offered her any.

For the past ten years, Ada had made the same trip alone. No one knew. She did not stay in the same cabin. She could not have borne that. Still, sometimes she did walk by to remember. She saw herself on her dad's lap on the deck, roasting marshmallows over the fire. She felt her mother's laughter as the water lapped up over her in the outdoor soaking tub beneath the stars. The cabin was always occupied, but if Ada hiked by at dusk, she could spy the antler chandelier and remember blanc de blanc on her tongue and her mother's operas. Back then in that tiny sphere of woods, there was no television, no computers, no phones—only books and pens and music.

Ada hummed her mom's song each pilgrimage. She sang where no one could hear her, see her, where there was not a trail. The first few trips out on her own she got lost.

Tall redwoods towered above. She wore a puffer coat and hiking boots and carried everything in a small backpack. The trips lasted a night at the most. It was the only way she did not have to explain to anyone. The next day she would drive or fly to celebrate Thanksgiving with friends, her trip locked away in her memory until the following year. Out of sight, out of touch, buried, burned, drowned, nonexistent.

Why she chose to return to a small sliver of her childhood to bury her grownup baggage she was not sure. She felt safe in there. The shade, the damp earth—so different than her beachside adolescence. She knew the ocean was still there. She felt it. She had grown up with it, in it, but she could not see it for the trees. These trees were all powerful. They towered above her, hundreds of years old, as wide as a Ritz Carlton suite, a hundred feet up, reaching to the sky Ada wished she could touch. It always seemed closer when she was in the ocean. Blue on blue, she felt surrounded on all sides.

But that pseudosafety was a long time ago. When her parents split up, they never went back. Ada's mom took Ada to visit various friends over Thanksgiving. The only tradition left to Ada was to leave home. New York, Hawaii, Florida. It changed every year, and it did not matter. Traditions were those of the friends they visited, none theirs. Her mom stopped writing on Thanksgiving. They did not take baths together or look up at the stars. Ada sat at the kids' table and then later made a game of meeting boys to pass the time wherever she went across the country. She would find them on palm tree-lined beaches, by walking someone's dog in the city or through playing rugby on the grass field in New England. At thirteen she started to love Thanksgiving again and never wanted to go back to the redwoods.

The desire to go back ten years ago at eighteen had surprised her, but the circumstances were very different, as were her motives. It was the only place she could think of that felt shielded, steady, unchanging.

Chris was the one who had given her the orange rose the first time. He took her to the airport, handed her the long-stemmed rose and kissed her on the cheek. She did not let herself cry. She thanked him, made a stupid joke, and got on the airplane. She let the rose dry out on her dresser. She took the petals and placed them in a small mason jar. She saved the petals until the next Thanksgiving break. She loaded up her Jeep and drove, stereo blaring. It took five hours. She kept a cooler full of iced tea, veggie wraps, and sunflower seeds in the trunk. She piled up the back seat with her duffel and blankets. The rose petals rode up front. Each year she took the velvety orange slips of beauty. Sometimes she bought the roses early to let the petals dry out. Sometimes she could not handle the sight of them so she would buy them fresh on the drive up. It started with one rose. Ada added one each year. She was up to ten.

The destination, a mile or so past the cabin, was a stone, nothing significant anyone but Ada would recognize. No human hands had hewn it into anything of consequence. There were no markings. A stone. Something to trod underfoot. No meaning. Just the hard dense slab—no feeling, no sound. The canopy of the trees stretched high above, a mosaic of moss below—myriad colors, hues, patterns, shapes. Ada lay her cheek on the cold, rough surface. She breathed in. She rarely cried, though part of her wanted to.

Each year she cleared the sticks away. One year there was a dead skunk. Ada did not care. She moved it to the river, threw it down the bank, and then returned to the stone. She sat there shaking, her body convulsing. She told herself that she would fulfill her word to be there, and she sat there until she felt a release. She threw her soiled clothes away before driving home.

The second year butterflies had covered the entire boulder. They were beautiful. Ada killed one. Dead. With her own hands. She held on to the beauty. Murder. Framed in glass in her bathroom at home. She normally left before dusk, but once she camped there overnight. She nearly froze. She told herself that she deserved it, and as soon as the sun came out ran the trail to her Jeep to blast the heater and find a warm cafe.

Each year she rubbed and rubbed the stone with a stick. She traced the word *ESTEL* over and over again. If she did this every year, one day Estel would become a part of the landscape. But the stick was powerless against the stone. Ada rubbed anyway. Only her memory was sharp. Too sharp. And this was the only place she was allowed to remember. Big Sur. What were you doing out here, Mom?

Ada sprayed herself with perfume as she stood naked in front of the mirror. She shivered though she still sweated from the scalding shower. She stared at herself as if looking at herself for the first time: large breasts, lean stomach, curved thighs, rounded ass. It was all the same, and yet it was not. Nothing had changed. Ada had. Her body had served her well, made her happy at times, but for the first time in a very long time she felt naked. She never felt naked, even when she was. Ada shivered again. Her body was her shield, not her vulnerability. She was exposed, and fearful her skin would reveal her secrets. Nathan saw through her. He made her feel. She never wanted a heart. Not now, not after how hard she had worked to get here.

Listen, it's easy when you don't exist. Then I win. I get what I want. Or at least it feels that way. I don't want to have a heart. I don't want to feel too deeply. It's easier not to. I want to laugh. I want to fuck. I want to be happy with myself, with you up inside of me, and then you going home. I don't want to want you to stay. If I want you to stay, then I'll lose control. Part of me dies in you. Because, really, you cannot save me—cannot be my everything. And if I love you it only reminds me that I am not good enough, not good enough for love. Sex is easy. Sex feels good. There is no shame. No pain. Please don't let me love you. Love is death.

Ada walked to the kitchen to pour herself a dusty *tempranillo*. She lit a cigarette and sat naked in the chaise lounge of the living room. She had already changed her dress four times. Nothing worked. She would be late, but she could not leave like this. Not yet. Fuck it all. She was stronger. She was not. She did not know. She could leave and not face it. No one else would ever know.

Ada blew smoke up at the chandelier and stared above her. Its crystal facets reflected the light through the open window. If she could just go to Nathan's flat tonight and see how ridiculous she was being about the whole thing, she could pack up her bags in the morning and finish up the rest of her trip in the south of France. She could stay up all night reading and then would have fulfilled her vow to herself and could leave it all behind once and for all to lie by the pool and drink champagne. No more Spanish.

Ada snuffed out her cigarette in the glass ashtray. She finished her wine as slowly as possible and then stood up to walk back into the bedroom closet. Conquer. What would she wear? She chose a simple red slip dress and flat snakeskin sandals. She looked in the mirror, smoothed her hair back and emphasized her lips with red lipstick. Easy, sexy, done.

She hailed a cab on the street. If she walked she would not make it. The driver stared at her from time to time in the rearview mirror. Instead of hiding her eyes on the passing buildings, she glared at him. She knew the way by memory—each stone, each curb, each tree. She jogged by, walked by, drove by, each time pretending that it did not matter, that because she could do this, be there, count the days forward, that it was no longer of consequence in her life. All the window shutters were the same—open with wrought-iron balconies. The stone facade was old, yet the building was modern. Nathan was at the top. Ada paid the driver and got out. This was it. It was almost over.

Ada buzzed number seventeen. The door vibrated, and she pushed. She looked up, breathed. There was the same elevator. Ada caught her reflection in the oversize mirror on the wall. She would take the stairs. Round and round, one step in front of the other. Ten years. Ten years was all. The carpet was new. She got to the tall, narrow, wooden door. She felt small. She reached for the handle and touched it softly, feeling, not wanting to. Did she have to? It was not safe. She should not be here. She turned to leave.

"Ada." Nathan called as she ran down the stairs. How did he know she was leaving? Why did he have to come out?

"I think I forgot something in the cab." Ada turned to look up at him.

"I'll be right back."

"Let me go. Door's open."

Nathan touched her arm as he passed her on the stairs. He ran down. Damn it. She turned and walked upward slowly, running her hand along the balustrade, and then touching the cool doorframe as she passed through. It was almost the same, only much more spare: the wooden floors, the stone walls, the exposed beams overhead. The floor plan was open. Nathan had removed some of the walls to make it feel like a loft after his grandmother's death. It had taken him a long time to go through her things. He was not someone to do anything without thinking it through from every angle.

Ada walked past the long, heavy, wood plank dining table, each side lined with five Fiancarlo Piretti plastic and steel folding chairs. She hadn't known what they were then. She did not remember the life-size canvas on the stone wall, either. It was dark, disturbing, the brushstrokes violent and unfinished, the canvas ripping from its frame. It did not seem like Nathan. She turned and then screamed as she found him directly behind her.

"Sorry." He put his hands on her arms. She looked at him and started laughing. "The cab was gone by the time I got down there. What was it that you left? We can call."

"No, it was nothing important. Thank you."

"Is it safe to gauge from your expression that this would not be gracing the presence of your apartment back home?"

"The painting? Well, who is the artist?"

"Does that make a difference?"

"Yes and no. It might help me understand it better."

"He was a friend. Last summer he jumped off the roof next door. His paintings are now worth a fortune. Fucking bastards. I won't sell it. He deserved more than that."

"What's it called?"

"Untitled. It's a piece from his first show, his only show."

"I'm sorry."

"It's all what we value. Art. Anyone with any real talent or with anything real worth saying is splattered down on that pavement outside, either literally or figuratively. You've either got to kill yourself or your soul to make it."

"But you haven't."

"And if my grandmother hadn't left me her flat, I'd be starving. But thanks to the good, honest work ethic of another generation, here I am. I have dinner up on the roof. You hungry?"

Ada wasn't thinking about food, but she told him she was hungry anyway. She wanted to explore the rest of the apartment, to sit in the same chair by the fireplace and run her fingers along the mortar between the rough stones of the walls. She followed Nathan. The

199

bedroom door was partially shut, and she could not see inside. She had spent little time on the roof before. Nathan slept up there while she was living with him. She did not like open places then. Nathan reached his hand down for Ada's as they reached the top of the spiral staircase.

"Gorgeous," Ada said. She scanned the views. "I had forgotten."

"I don't remember you coming up here."

"You brought me up here once." Ada blushed. This made her blush more. Why was she blushing? She wasn't afraid to be seen.

"Well I hope your culinary tastes haven't changed too much. I remember you being quite adamantly Mediterranean, so I made a picnic for us. Lots of calamari, olives, tomatoes, wine."

"May I start with some wine?" Ada interrupted. She sat down on one of the long flat sofas that ran the length of the space. She set her clutch down on the soft white fabric and watched Nathan select a bottle from the ice bucket beneath the low wooden table.

"I'd figured you'd graduated from Diet Coke and rum," Nathan said. Ada laughed. "You had a running order back then. When you went back to California, Bernat from the liquor store was hurting for business."

"Oh my god, I remember that well." Ada laughed harder. "You were always a good sport about my whims and addictions."

"You cost me a fortune in cigarettes," Nathan said. He handed her a glass of cava.

"*Gràcies*. And that's all I remember in *Catalàn*," Ada said. She clinked glasses with Nathan, stared directly up into his eyes and took a sip. It was dry, crisp, grapefruit and fresh herbs, like her grandmother's summer garden. "This is actually really good."

"I knew you were a wine snob by now." Nathan sat down next to her. He smelled like something from far away, something Ada had forgotten existed—something that made her cross her legs and try to remember. "You must be a champagne aficionada."

"Guilty," Ada said. She looked at him out of the corner of her eye and took another sip. "How do you know that?"

"I'm not even going to answer that," Nathan said. He squeezed her knee and lay back on the sofa. "There are good cavas now, if you know where to look."

"I have only drunk Spanish wines since I got here. It's a reawakening."

"I always thought you'd come back."

"Here?"

"To Barcelona. Or maybe you have. You didn't give me a call this trip."

"No, I didn't, but no, I haven't. It's been ten years."

"Ten years. Wow. Well, by looking at you they were good to you."

"And you. I read your book."

"Which one? The book of poetry or the analysis of existentialist literature of post-Civil War Spain?"

"Take a wild guess."

"And?"

"Your poetry is brilliant. Scary, but beautiful."

"But your poem?"

"My poem?"

"Number 18. You didn't know it was you I was talking about?"

"Me?"

"You're shivering." Nathan took one of Ada's hands in between his and rubbed it. "I have a bottle of Vega Sicilia Unico in my study. Let's go downstairs, and I'll light a fire for us."

35

Nathan flipped on the lamp in the study. She wanted him so badly. Why didn't he want her? She was throbbing, and when nothing happened, her chest felt like it had a huge hole. Empty. This was empty. Fuck this. It was not worth it. Nathan went to a cabinet in the corner. Ada watched him select a wine bottle and then turned her eyes away.

"You still have this."

Ada picked up the old brass kaleidoscope off the long 1950s Borsani conference table Nathan used as his dining table and sometimes desk. Books were stacked on each end, papers were scattered throughout, and a thin, large laptop was folded closed in front of one of the leather executive chairs. Ada twisted the kaleidoscope around without looking inside. She listened to the familiar clink as the colorful images changed. Still she did not look.

"That was my grandmother's," Nathan said. "We used to play a game with it the one summer I stayed with her when I was a boy. My parents toured the Mediterranean and left me here. I was six, maybe. I had never met my grandmother before, so I was scared. I was shy anyway, and she only spoke in Catalonian. I don't think I talked all summer except when we played the game."

"You were shy?" Ada asked. "I find that hard to believe. You always seem to have a lot to say."

"But is it worth saying?" Nathan asked. He looked at Ada and laughed. "I think a lot. Too much. Back then I kept all my thoughts inside, trapped in a whirlwind. Never slept much. Now I think them aloud and just don't give a damn. Not that anything I say is worth listening to."

"I always found you interesting."

"You were eighteen."

"I'm not anymore."

"Then I take that as a huge compliment coming from you. Play the game with me."

"Teach me."

"Let's go sit by the fire," Nathan said. They walked into the living room. Ada turned her back to the painting in the dining room and sat down on the dark Moroccan rug. She traced the star pattern of the wool with her finger as Nathan made up the fire. "I'd get in bed, and my grandmother would pull the sheet up over me. I was hot, but she made me wear long-sleeved pajamas, and she kept the window closed. She would hand me the kaleidoscope and tell me to twist it. I did whatever she said as best as I could. She would always look in it first, and without making any expression that I could understand, she would point and tell me to look inside. Then she'd ask me to tell her what I saw and what each part meant."

"You go first," Ada said. Nathan sat down next to her, and she handed him the kaleidoscope. He twisted it and put it back in her hand. She looked inside. Ada thought of the ocean—blues, greens, depths, variations. And then there was the occasional white, like the clouds scattered across a bright, clean sky. She tried not to make an expression as she handed it to Nathan. He took it and looked inside. He then set the kaleidoscope down on the rug between them and looked Ada in the eyes as he thought.

"At sixteen years old, I took my first road trip. My buddy Will and I had just gotten our licenses, and it was a long weekend. We took a couple other friends—girls, of course—down the coast in Will's Grand Cherokee. It was the most fun I had ever had in my life for forty-eight hours. We took turns driving, sang, told dirty jokes, stopped where we wanted, drank whiskey the blonde had in her purse. We stayed at a dive motel and had our eyes opened. We were young. We got up and kept driving. We never stopped to think, to take our time, to sleep it off. I honestly still don't remember who was driving when we crashed. I remember it being me, but the investigation said otherwise. I only know that I was the only one who lived to remember anything."

"Jesus, that's terrible. I am so sorry."

"It taught me to enjoy and respect life. I spent a lot of time trying to get those days back—the innocence is bliss, pretraumatic life lesson days. But then I realized there was no virtue in sorrow. And as hard as I tried, I had no power to change what had happened. One day I woke up, chose to be happy and to live every last day of this fucking fantastic, horrific, beautiful, upside-down life."

"And you're doing a good job."

"Your turn."

Ada picked up the kaleidoscope and twisted it several times. She handed it to Nathan. He looked inside and then his expression was blank as he handed it back to her. She took a deep breath and looked inside. No. She did not want this. What happened to all of the colors? Why were there only jagged edges? Everything was orange and black, the occasional red triangle rimming the bold pattern.

"I want to retwist."

"Against the rules."

"We can change them."

"Why do you think that?"

"It's ugly."

"Not with this kaleidoscope."

"You look good in orange."

"Because it's orange."

"I don't wear orange."

"You used to. Ada, what do you see inside of here?"

Ada paused. She didn't want to tell him. All she saw was sex. But not the good kind. Not the kind where she was in complete control. Not the kind where she knew exactly how to move her body to get what she wanted. This was the wrong kind of sex. The kind that was rough, but not rough because she wanted it that way up on the bar or bent over the balcony. This was so rough it was lined in blood. It was dark, black, cold. She had no control.

"I see black flies on fresh orange halves. They are on a plate on a counter outside. There is a hand, but I don't know whose it is. It's young, with nails freshly manicured in red. There is maybe a party because there is a table laid out for breakfast by the pool. The tablecloth is ironed. There are roses on the table. Coffee is brewing. But then the hand picks up the orange and twists it to make juice. It's black. But the black juice won't stop. It keeps pouring out of the bowl until the whole table is covered in black. The party is over before it ever began."

Ada looked away from the flames of the fire and into Nathan's eyes. She immediately looked away. What the fuck was she saying? He kept his eyes on her. He pushed one of her messy curls out of her eye. They sat there silently. Sex was easy. Love was hard. Ada did not want anyone to see her, and she felt that cold knife again. Her head bashed on the sidewalk. She shivered.

"I don't believe in love," Ada said.

"Okay," Nathan said. "And how many men have told you they love you?"

"I don't ask them to love me."

"They can't help it. They do."

"But they don't, really. They think they do. I understand that. I'm not callous about it, but it's not love. I'm their muse, or they love some idea of me. It's an image, a dream, an idea. It's not real."

"They love you, Ada."

"They don't even know me," Ada said. She started to cry. She got up. Nathan grabbed her hand and pulled her back to the rug. "I need to go."

"What is it that they don't know?"

"You know. My god, you know more about me than anyone. How many stories about my life have I told you? And you never loved me. How could you?"

"How could I? Ada, you were eighteen years old when I found you."

"Stop."

"When I found you, you were——"

"Stop!"

"You were almost dead."

"That did not happen, Nathan."

"I don't know what happened or what didn't happen. You never told me. I do know what happened earlier that night and then what happened after I found you."

"Well, that's because nothing happened. And I never met you beforehand, anyway."

"Ada, I watched you from the moment you walked into that club. Your hair was long and so blonde. You looked like you had been out in the sun all day the way you glowed. You had on that dress. It was orange with flowers up the side. When you danced, it would swing around your thighs. It was very short. And I remember your smile. You smiled from the moment you walked in and down those stairs, totally oblivious to anything around you but the music."

"You saw me?"

"Of course I saw you. You were gorgeous, Ada."

"Why didn't you talk to me?"

"I just wanted to watch you dance. You were so happy. When I found you . . ."

"Stop. Don't. It's done. I fucked everything up."

"You didn't do anything wrong, Ada."

"It's my fault. I never should have stepped into that elevator."

"I don't know about should or shouldn't. I do know that if I had ever caught the fucking bastard that did that to you, he wouldn't be alive right now. So maybe it's better I found you alone and in time to get you help. I can't even see your scars."

"It wasn't just one," Ada said, more to herself than to Nathan.

"What?"

"Nothing. I don't really remember that part, but I know I owe you a lot for what you did."

"I only did what was right."

"Maybe I got what I deserved."

"You can't be serious, Ada. You deserved none of that. Do you hear me? I can't even imagine the pain you must have been in. I swear I thought you were dead. I have never seen that much blood."

"Nathan, I don't feel well. Do you think I can sleep here tonight?"

"Of course. You take the bedroom. I'll sleep up on the roof. And, Ada, nothing about you is bad. I know you. You want to feel good, to have peace, to be free. Whoever cannot understand that is confused. Feel your way out. You know the way."

Ada walked down the dark hallway. She ran her fingertips along the rough texture of the creamy walls. Jasmine perfumed the air. The balcony was left open. A warm breeze wafted through the bedroom. Ada paused in the doorway. She breathed in and sighed. The dim streetlights cast eerie yet familiar shadows on the floorboards. Ada stepped inside. The floor creaked underfoot. As Ada passed the plush bed she caught the reflection of her silhouette in the long mirror. She was here. She walked to the wall of books and felt the myriad musty pages. She breathed in the scent of must, jasmine, and tempranillo, and then pulled the cord to light the bedside lamp.

She walked over to the balcony to flip the old radio on. No fucking way. That song. Why did it get so much airtime? She walked back to lie down on the feather mattress. She turned the lamp off and stared up at the ceiling. Why would they play this song? It took her back to the first time she ever heard Rihanna. Pain. Raw. My heart in my hand. Held up. A child. An offering. Why are they playing this song here? Blood. Like being fucked over and over again. Wait. The world was beautiful. Dancing. Burning lungs. Breath. No. Happily ever after. Fun. It could be. What are you doing? Don't fucking touch me. Asshole. Bastards. Get your dirty hands off me. You can go fuck yourselves. No. Eyes. Dark, light. Hands. Large, strong. Fury. Domination. Glazed over. Lust. I will fuck you from behind and then whip you over and fuck you from the front. Ripped skin. Pounding heart. Alive. Shut your fucking, screaming mouth. I will choke you. Harder. My left hand is tight on your neck, gripping, closing off your throat. Voiceless. My right hand in your mouth. Bitch, don't bite me. I'll whack your head harder next time. Do you feel me inside of you? Yeah, you do. Jesus, you feel good. My angel. Blondes look good in red. Just don't get it on me. I don't know where you've been. Is that my blood?

Ada rolled over and opened her eyes. Books. Nameless pages. No. Yes. What? Had she really slept there? She slept? For how long? She was naked. She was alone. She traced Nathan's initials on the pillowcase. She was starving. She was terrified. But she slept. And she woke up again. She let herself remember.

The club was crazy fabulous. Ada felt the music vibrate through her. Hell, yes. Why weren't her friends here? This was insane. Whatever, she would have fun without them. Sarah was always so high and mighty, and it's not like Ada needed a designated driver. Fuck that. Ada could take care of herself. She was there to have fun, and she could tell by the music there was no doubt about that. It was 1:30 a.m. and people were just starting to arrive. She had been warned by her bunkmate in the nearby hostel that no one would be out any earlier. She had set her alarm for half-past midnight so she would have all the energy she wanted to dance all night. But first she wanted a drink.

The club was spread out over several levels—the pool, the palm trees, the Mediterranean, the multistory indoor dance floors. Ada checked it all out, only semioblivious to the stares that followed her as she moved about. She could think about that later. It was too early to single anyone out. The night was young and better would be coming later. Ada circled the long rectangular pool of the terrace to get to the bar closest to the ocean. She felt the warm night air on her skin. Guys made comments and whistles as she passed by. She was hot, and she knew it. College was going to be so much fun.

"What are you drinking?" the barman asked in Catalan. Ada did not need a translation.

"Rum and Diet Coke," she said. She reached into her bra for her ID and cash.

The barman shook his head. It had already been paid for. Ada smiled, glanced around for a second, and before she could make eye contact with anyone, walked away, sipping her drink. She walked toward a group of tanned travelers in their early twenties.

"Great dress," one of the girls said as Ada walked past.

"Where are you from?" Ada turned and asked. She stopped and took a cigarette from one of the guys wearing cargo shorts and a white T-shirt.

"Australia," the girl on his arm in short pink shorts answered as she looked Ada over. "You?"

"California," Ada said as she began to smoke. "What are you all doing in Barcelona?"

"We studied spring semester abroad at the University of Salamanca, but we're taking the summer to backpack about before we go home."

"Cool," Ada said, then blew out smoke as one of the taller guys handed her a fresh drink. "I just got to Barcelona. How do you like it?"

"Craziest parties. The most fun ever!" the redhead in the silver tank said.

"You find a party anywhere," the girl in the pink shorts said. "You can't even remember half of what you do. Next week, Berlin will be the best."

"It really is the best here," the redhead said. She stared at Ada and winked before taking her hand as she began to dance. "You'll never want to leave this place."

They danced outside by the pool and drank a few rounds together, but before long Ada was bored with her new friends. She did not want to hear anyone talk, especially not in English. She only wanted the music. She wanted it to vibrate through her so hard and heavy that no thoughts came, only movement.

She motioned to Katie that she was going to the bar for another drink. Instead she went inside to get closer to the DJ. This is where she wanted to be. It was packed, sweaty. Ada loved it. She danced her way into the center of the crowd. She slapped someone who grabbed her ass. She hoped she hit the right person. Oh well, it didn't matter now. She was moving, moving. Someone's hands were on her waist. He was tall, Norwegian maybe. Whatever. She did not care. He pulled her tight up against himself. He was sweaty and smelled like the beach. So happy. She ground on him until the song ended and then pulled herself away without looking back to move deeper into the crowd.

Life was fucking amazing. Hands, bodies, breathlessness. Oh my god, that guy is so smoking hot right there. Jesus, he looked like Chris only with darker skin and lighter green eyes. She stared straight at him as she flipped her long hair over her shoulders and danced up on him. He was not a good dancer, but oh my god those lips, and his hands. Viva Barcelona. Ada reached up and kissed him. Her tongue slipped into his mouth and played the game she did with it. Damn, his hands were strong, but wait, just another second more. Yes. She finally pulled away and laughed. She winked and blew him a kiss good-bye. He grabbed her, but she shook her head and pulled away hard. She wanted to dance upstairs on one of those platforms.

How would she get up there? Oh wait, there were the stairs behind the bar. These heels were killing her, but it didn't matter. They were half a size too small. She had taken them from her mom's girlfriend's closet and thrown them in her suitcase the night she left for Europe. Carrie had amazing taste. Ada's system was normally flawless. She knew how to put things back exactly how Carrie displayed them in the large walk-in closet, but this time she would know these were missing. Ada knew she would be pissed, but she would not say a thing to her mom. She was still trying to get on Ada's good side.

A shot? Yes, absolutely. Thank you. No, just once. The stairs. Where were the stairs? What? No, I have no idea what you are saying. I'm not Russian. Californian. Seriously. I don't know Russian. Fuck you. I want to go dance. Oh, good. There are the stairs. Oh my god! Don't cha wish your girlfriend was hot like me? Perfect. What? No, I'm not here alone. I'm going upstairs to meet my friends. No, don't waste your time. I'm the ugly duckling of the group. Go, Ada, go. Almost there. Look at the crowd from up here. Spain was the best place ever.

Ada danced on one of the platforms that overlooked the dance floor. She could feel the energy of the bodies below. Everywhere she looked there were new faces, energy to feed off of as she went wild on her stage. Freedom. Movement. Life. To this moment. An hour passed.

Sweat ran between her breasts. Her legs burned. Her throat was raw from singing. It was time for another drink. But first the bathroom.

Ada waited in the long line of the coed bathroom. She did not realize how bad she needed to pee. She had been so absorbed in the music she had forgotten about her body outside of its movement. There was no way she could make it. Shit. She pushed past the crowd in front of her, entered the littered bathroom, and walked toward the sink. She turned the water on, running her hands under the faucet, pretending to wash her hands as she awaited her opportunity. A tall, bearded Spaniard came out of the stall behind her and Ada slipped inside and turned the latch before anyone else could. Someone pounded on the door and swore at her in Catalan, but Ada could not care less. She already had pulled her panties down to her knees and was squatting over the toilet.

When she came out, the Spaniard was waiting for her by the sink. She walked over to the basin and glanced at him before turning on the faucet and washing her hands again. There was probably no point. There was no soap, and sanitation did not seem possible. She ran her hands under the trickling water in a trance until the Spaniard turned it off and took her hand. His skin was olive, his eyes deep and dark. He led Ada outside of the bathroom and down the hallway. She pulled in the other direction to head back to her dance perch, but he shook his head and touched her nose with his finger.

"Coca," he said, and kept walking.

Ada glanced up at him and wavered. Coke wasn't her thing—only sometimes, anyway. She did not need it. But why not? This was a special night—a night to celebrate her freedom. Cocaine. A gorgeous man in his twenties. The Mediterranean. Killer DJ. Yes.

He led her into an elevator. She did not notice it was a service elevator until she was inside. Weird. Maybe he works here. He pushed the button for the basement. Maybe there was an underground club underneath the club. That made sense. She liked being on the inside. He put his hands around her waist and pulled her up onto him. She would kiss him once and then leave once the elevator doors opened. He looked like a novella star, but she did not like his smell. She wanted to go dance. She needed the music. He put his hand up under her dress and started running his hand up her thigh. She pushed his hand away. Stop. He grabbed her dress and with a sudden, painful movement ripped it off her. What the fuck? You can go to hell, asshole. He whacked her head against the mirror to the side of her. She felt blood trickle down her temple. The doors opened, and there they were. Waiting just for her.

36

"Good afternoon," Nathan said as Ada walked into the kitchen. He motioned for her to sit down where he had breakfast laid out for her. Coffee, orange juice, *pa amb tomaquet. It was the same.*

"What happened to my dress?" Ada asked.

"On the sofa," Nathan said as he poured her coffee. "My old Stanford T-shirt looks the best it ever has all faded on your body, but I can lend you something else if you want to shower."

"No, not the dress I wore here. The dress from that night. The orange one with the flowers."

"I don't know. You weren't wearing it when I found you in the alleyway."

Ada sat down on one of the midcentury swivel bar stools. She lifted her glass and took a sip of orange juice. She stared at Nathan. He leaned against the butcher-block counter and looked back at her. Neither of them spoke for a long time. Nathan walked over and wrapped his arms around her. She rested her head on his stomach and started to cry. This time she did not stop herself. She just cried, not wiping away the tears. Not stopping them, not fighting them. She let herself feel. Hurt. Could she admit that to herself? Vacant, cold, terrifying. Feeling. This feeling. Nathan did not let her go. They just stayed there. Was it ten minutes or an hour? She breathed in and out with him, listening to his heart beat. Fuck. She had forgotten all these feelings. Okay. Okay. She finally put her hand on his arm and looked up at him.

"I have something that you should have," Nathan told her.

He took her hand and walked her down the hallway to his study. Nothing had changed. Maybe the plants had grown. Maybe some had been replaced. But the feeling was the same. The books, the mirror, the fireplace, the worn Berber rug, the guitar in the corner. Ada felt safe and afraid at the same time. Nathan stopped beside Ada against his desk. She did not see him motion to the old apothecary jar. Ada picked up a pile of worn photos instead. She began to flip through them. Some of them Ada had taken when she was first learning photography that summer with Nathan. Some of them were from other places Ada did not recognize. One of them was of a woman.

"Who is this?" Ada asked.

"That's Catherine."

"Nathan, I am so sorry."

"Why are you sorry?"

"Because you loved her."

"I did love her. That's nothing to be sorry for."

"But she broke your heart."

"Ada, where is this coming from? I did love Catherine, Ada, but not enough."

"Not enough?"

"Catherine did not break my heart. I broke hers. And, yeah, the guilt ate me up."

"But she left you."

"Who told you that? I am the one who is sorry. I must have been odious for you to live with. I apologize for being so melancholy during those months you were with me. It took me a while to move on and forgive myself."

"Wait. She didn't leave you? What did you do to her?"

"You are still Ada, aren't you?" Nathan took the photos out of Ada's hand, set them back down on the desk, and then looked her in the eyes. "I cheated on her. It was stupid and thoughtless on my part. Catherine was worth ten times more than any woman I have met since, present company excluded, of course."

"You cheated on her?"

"Guilty."

"But you were perfect."

"Wow, how many times did they hit you on the head, Ada?" Ada looked down. He put his finger on her chin and pulled her gaze back up to his.

"Hey, bad joke. There is nothing wrong with that head of yours."

Then she saw it. The photo. Her first show. The show that had paid for her move to San Francisco. The show Jordan had said was not real. The show that he made her have and then told her that made her a sellout. The show that was buried so deeply in a world of dreams that Ada could rarely access anymore. But how? On Nathan's desk was a photo Ada had taken. Yes. She recognized the alleyway she had chosen, the alleyway called Garden of My Love.

The blood on her lips was real. Dismembered mannequins, male and female, lay in a smoky pile on the asphalt beside her. Her thin, silk, leopard-print slip dress, ripped down the front, revealed bloodied breasts. The textured men's blazer from London, scuffed and splotched in red. Her bare feet facing the lens, perfect pedicure, lifeless feet. Crucified. Baked on the asphalt in the heat of the day. Siesta. Her sharp stilettos pierced through her outstretched palms.

But no. Jordan had never seen these. Wait. That was never at the show. No one had ever seen the images she shot in the alleyway or the poems she wrote on the back of the photographs. She never published those photos. They were only for her. She picked up the double pressed glass frame to turn it over. It was her handwriting in a thin black Sharpie: *Do we fear our own reality? Are we ashamed? Of what? Rejection? I am not perfect. We call it reality.*

"Where did you get this?"

"I bought it."

"How?"

"Through my dealer."

"Fuck."

"Ada."

"No."

"Ada."

She ran out without ever seeing her python earrings in the apothecary jar on his desk.

37

Ada walked into the orange-tiled bathroom of her apartment and shut the door. She took a deep breath and stared down at her polished toenails. One, two three … She locked the door behind her and walked over to the shower. She turned the cold water on full blast. She dipped her feet under the water one by one and listened to the downpour from above her head as she continued to focus on her breathing. Four, five, six … The muggy bathroom began to drop in temperature. Ada soaked her legs, washed her hands, and ran her hands through her hair. She climbed up onto the tile counter and straddled the sink.

One breath at a time.

I see you, Ada. Cool, clear eyes. Are you ready to talk?

I don't need to talk. I just need to cool down.

Then just sit here.

It's not a big deal, you know. I'm just hot … and bored … and fucking annoyed. I don't even know why I'm here. There's nothing to do, nothing to prove. I'm going to pack first thing tomorrow morning. I have friends in France.

You have friends everywhere.

I do.

You do.

Jesus, I just want to be alone for once, though, and to be okay being alone.

You are okay.

No I'm not.

Why aren't you?

You fucking know why.

Tell me.

Those assholes.

What assholes?

I used to be real, alive. I could see a lifetime in a branch, the sun shining on the leaves. Now I move, I go, I wander, I breathe, I drink, I fuck, and I conquer. But a single slow breath, the fairies? Dance.

Not now . . .

You still dance.

It's not the same.

How many were there?

Four, five maybe.

Tell me what happened to you.

Nothing happened to me.

Then dance.

Dance? Right now?

To Rihanna.

Fuck you.

Ada climbed down off the counter. She walked down the hallway to the living room and pushed the large coffee table off to one side. She pulled the chaise lounge over to the windows and then unlatched each of them, one by one. She was sweating again, but she wanted to feel the street air on her skin. She pulled her dress up over her head and walked into the kitchen in her lace bra and panties. She opened the refrigerator and poured what remained of the bottle of the Vega Sicilia tempranillo from the night before. She placed the stem between her breasts and took a breath. She stuck her nose in the glass and breathed. She then drank the dark fruit and cedar in, swirling the fleshy wine around her mouth as she contemplated her next move. Music. Move, Ada.

She swirled her glass around again. Long legs ran down the glass, thick, alluvial, like blood mixed with earth. She took another sip. I am not afraid of you. You will not beat me. Rhythm, control, abandon. Fuck it. She turned the recording on. Music flooded the room. Turn it up. She took another sip—tobacco, dusty blackberries—and set her glass down on the coffee table. She felt the first finger pickings. Come in. She was wet. She took off her bra and straddled the chaise lounge. She fell back, arching her back as she slipped off her panties. She stretched her legs out long, letting one after the other fall off the side of the chaise. The floorboards were cool. She was sweating. The strumming came faster, almost frenzied. Where were those fucking shoes? I will do this.

She reached under the chaise. Found them. She ran her fingers along the nail heads of the heels and read the grail of her soul.

What were the lyrics?

They threw me into the sea.

Well, I am not a gypsy. I am fucking Ada, and they threw me into a Dumpster.

Give me the sea.

Cover me in salt and waves.

Let me feel the burn in slit skin.

Wash the blood out of my hair, the saliva off my nipples, the semen out of my mouth.

Freedom? What is freedom?

I am Ada. I want to breathe. I want my lungs to burn with life. I want to run naked on a hot beach, to feel the waves on my body. I want to fuck the sun, the moon, and all the stars. I want to feel the universe on top of me. I want to melt into the earth until I am devoured, to be no more, just enveloped in her presence. I want to burst into a million pieces, to float, to feel the power of myriad atoms and galaxies and the nameless. And then, when I am ready, I want to solidify in to this shaking body. I will breathe, raised from the dead.

She stomped hard. Fury was not enough. Move feet. Bleed. Crush. She clapped her hands, softly in rhythm, then harder. Make it burn. I want to feel. Let me feel it. The cold fear. What? Where am I? Why are you doing this to me? The pain. The counter against my skull. Wait. Please. Stop. The knives between my legs, the force up my ass. Oh my god. No. Please. The blur. My blood running down my forehead, my eyes. I can't see. You're going to kill her. Someone is coming. Hide her. Take her out back. Oh Jesus. Cold. Wait, I am alive. Fuck no, please no. Not more. Let me die.

38

Ada paced the apartment at dawn. When her eyes finally registered on Nathan's old, red T-shirt on the coffee table, she ran to the closet in search of her backpack. Ada dumped it upside down and rummaged frantically through her things in search of a pack of cigarettes. She then continued to pace the apartment, cigarettes in hand, finally throwing the pack out the window before she could find a lighter. Ada watched the pack hit the sidewalk below. The cigarettes rolled along the tree-lined street, one falling into the gutter. Ada sat on the windowsill to stare further, her eyes focused on the one solitary tube of white in the gutter, now dirty and exposed.

Ada wept. The first few tears traveled slowly down her cheeks, and she wiped them away quickly. Soon her eyes were blurred until she could no longer see the cigarette below. She turned to pull her head back into the apartment and stumbled over to slump down into the chaise lounge. She picked up the shirt. The worn cotton was soft in her grip. She lifted it up to smell it and threw it down onto the rug. She stared at the kaleidoscope. She had run out with it. She grabbed it. It was cold in her palms. She turned it round and round without looking into it. Ada knew what she would see inside. She then began to sob, her gasps for air becoming louder and louder until she finally screamed angrily to stop herself from crying anymore.

Ada stood and took slow, determined steps until she reached the bedroom. Reaching the threshold, she forced herself to continue onward to the nightstand, staring at the worn orange leather of the journal. She set the kaleidoscope down, and her hand trembled to pick the journal up. Ada took a pen from the drawer and flung herself onto the bed. She lay on her stomach and opened the journal to the first blank page.

Please take my masks off, all of them, and if you see the monster beneath the goddess's façade, kill her.

And after that, when she has been destroyed and is no more, could you still love me? The smallness of what will be left is insignificant ashes. If you blew on the ashes, could they ever reignite? Instead of an inferno of destruction, could I ever become a blaze of beauty and light?

This is the question I am desperate to find the answer to: Can anyone love me? Can I love myself?

Ada closed her journal. She ran her finger down the spine. All the words she had ever written only filled up a third of the pages. She threw it in her Birkin and left the apartment. She began to walk, seeing nothing but color, hearing nothing but faraway echoes, stopping in a mile when another step in snakeskin stilettos became unbearable. Ada had thrown on what she could grab the fastest: black miniskirt, thin tank, an oversize denim jacket. She was lucky she was wearing anything on her feet at all. The python heels were an afterthought in the stairwell. Ada hailed a cab and whispered *Parc Güell* to the driver. She took her journal and pen from her bag and kept writing.

Why did you show up like that? You knew what I was, what I'd sell out for. How hard I tried, how brutally I failed. It never did matter how hard I tried, really. I always fucked up. Always. I did want to be good. I once did want to make everyone proud. Of course I did. I don't know why I couldn't be good or normal, why I can't be now. But you showed up out of nowhere. Broke open my door. You told me I was more. You saved me. I don't even believe in saviors, but you are mine.

The taxi stopped and Ada slammed the journal closed. She handed the driver a wad of euros and climbed out onto the pavement into a group of singing schoolchildren. Ada zigzagged her way through the uniforms until she reached the staircase. She looked toward the columns up above. Ada climbed up slowly, past Python, past tourists, past tour guides, past a dozen clicking cameras. Smile. Focus. Walk. She reached the landing and crossed into the shade. There were eighty-six Doric columns to wind between. She wandered past the couple with toddler twins, past the ten-year-old violin virtuoso, past the blonde kissing the brunette on the other side of the column from their friends. Ada found the darkest column of the eighty-six. She slid her back down the white mosaic and looked upward. More tiles. White, rainbow colors, popped bubbles, the world caving in and then popping right back out again.

Can you be real? Can love? I laugh at it. How can it be? People change. I do. Well, not exactly, I am always the same. Same DNA, same spirit, same overriding purpose. But I am infinite. I may take on different masks. One facade one day, another facet the next. It's uncanny, brilliant, terrifying, but it's all me. The myriad interpretations are never ending. So love? Unconditional? What does that even mean? Kaleidoscopic color. That's me. That's you.

Ada tossed her things back in her bag and stood up. She brushed her legs off and stretched upward before walking back out toward the light. Ada reached the staircase and there he was. Nathan was standing right there. Right in front of her. Right past Python, the guardian of subterranean waters. Fuck it all. Maybe being loved did not matter. Maybe only loving did. It felt like freedom. Love. No deficit. Overflow.

"Ada." Nathan looked at her. "I know a really great Italian place."

"Oh, really?"

"Do you want to go get some spaghetti? You choose the wine."

"As long as I can bring my camera."

About the Author

At seventeen, Tyler Kyle began traveling through Europe where she lived and worked in a castle in Austria. She continued to Russia, Israel, and finally, Spain. Tyler earned her master of arts in Spanish from California State University, Sacramento, and master of arts in teaching from the University of Southern California. Tyler is a certified French and American wine scholar, an Italian wine professional, and currently studies Spanish vintages. She is a yoga instructor in downtown Napa, California, where she lives with her twin daughters and French bulldog.

Edwards Brothers Malloy
Ann Arbor MI. USA
April 25, 2017